I0451434

FOR A LITTLE WHILE

• • •

ONE STRIKE AWAY BOOK ONE

• • •

MARY J. WILLIAMS

Copyright © 2017 by Mary J. Williams.

All Rights Reserved. No part of this publication may be copied, reproduced in any format, by any means, electronic or otherwise, without prior consent from the Copyright owner and publisher of this book.

First Ebook Printing, 2017

ABOUT THE AUTHOR

Writing isn't easy. But I love every second. A blank screen isn't the enemy. It is the opportunity to create new friends and take them on amazing adventures and life-changing journeys. I feel blessed to spend my days weaving tales that are unique—because I made them.

Billionaires. Songwriters. Artists. Actors. Directors. Stuntmen. Football players. They fill the pages and become dear friends I hope you will want to revisit again and again.

Thank you for jumping into my books and coming along for the journey.

HOW TO GET IN TOUCH

Please visit me at these sites, sign up for my newsletter or leave a message.

http://www.maryjwilliams.net/

https://www.facebook.com/maryjwilliamsauthor/?ref=hl

https://twitter.com/maryjwilliams05

https://www.pinterest.com/maryj0675/

https://www.instagram.com/2015romance/

https://www.goodreads.com/author/show/5648619.Mary_J_Willia ms

MORE BOOKS BY MARY J. WILLIAMS

Harper Falls Series

If I Loved You

If Tomorrow Never Comes

If You Only Knew

If I Had You (Christmas in Harper Falls)

Hollywood Legends Series

Dreaming with a Broken Heart

Dreaming with My Eyes Wide Open

Dreaming Again

Dreaming of a White Christmas

(Caleb and Callie's story)

One Pass Away Series

After the Rain

After All These Years

After the Fire

Hart of Rock and Roll

Flowers on the Wall

Flowers and Cages

Flowers are Red

Flowers for Zoe

WITH ONE MORE LOOK AT YOU

TABLE OF CONTENTS

CHAPTER ONE

WHOEVER SAID PERFECT was boring had never met Spencer Kraig.

The man was the epitome of tall, dark, and handsome. Charismatic. Well spoken. Well read. Smooth. Whether hobnobbing with the rich and famous or making a jaw-dropping defensive play at third base, he never put a foot wrong.

However, it would be a mistake to assume Spencer Kraig was a vapid pretty boy whose personality had long ago been polished to a shiny gleam. There were edges under his suit. Sharp. On rare occasions—if pushed too far—dangerous.

A sense of fun shone from Spencer's dark green eyes. A natural charm drew people to him. When he played, he played hard. His adventures were legendary. Some small. Some big. But always—in every way—he made life a blast.

Spencer had his pick of women. His circle of friends was wide and varied. Though make no mistake, he was discerning when it came to all aspects of his life. Private and professional. He had a strict motto—a bit of advice from his father he'd never forgotten.

Choose your friends, lovers, and business associates wisely. The character of the people who surround you says as much about you as it does about them.

Spencer Kraig lived his life in a way that made it impossible to find anything to criticize. He was walking, talking perfection in a six-foot-three-inch drool-worthy package. The world loved the Seattle Cyclones' third baseman.

But the world didn't include Blue O'Hara.

"I hate that man."

Picking up the remote, Blue turned off the television with a decisive jab. *Damn Mercedes commercial.* The thing was on constantly. Bad enough that she couldn't go anywhere in this city without seeing the jerk's smiling face. Billboards. Buses. He loomed over her or sped past no matter what corner she turned.

Where was it written that Spencer Kraig was allowed to invade the sanctity of Blue's home as well?

"You don't hate Spencer."

Crap! Blue had meant to keep the comment to herself. Now she had no choice but to do what she always did. Barrel ahead.

"Yes. I do, Jordyn. I have every right to hate the jackass," she said to the woman who was currently sprawled on her sofa drinking a glass of very fine Chardonnay.

"It's your right. I'll give you that." Jordyn stretched out her long legs, wiggling her bright pink-tipped toes. "The problem is this. If you hate Spencer, it's my obligation—as your best friend—to feel the same. One of those pesky unwritten rules."

"I'm a big fan of unwritten rules."

"However," Jordyn soldiered on, ignoring Blue. "I can't hate

Spencer."

"You could try."

"Nope."

"But—"

Jordyn held up a hand, cutting Blue off before she began. "Do you want me to run down the list?"

"No."

"Number one."

Blue groaned. "I said no."

"Number one." Jordyn held up a finger. "He loves dogs and children."

"That hardly makes him a saint."

Why were they doing this? Blue practically knew the list by heart. She should. Jordyn recited it often enough.

"Number two. He gives back to his community. Often without any recognition."

Fine, Blue thought as she plopped down in the overstuffed recliner. She'd give the guy props for that one. Spencer Kraig believed in helping his fellow man. Those less fortunate. He spread around his time and money with a liberal hand. Often with as low a profile as possible.

"Number three. How can you hate a face like that?" Jordyn took a magazine from the coffee table—the one with the cover face down—turning it over. "Such an angelic expression."

A fallen angel. And a damned sexy one. Blue refused to admit that to anybody—but herself.

"Numbers four through eight. And these are the true sticking points." Jordyn held up her fingers, counting down with each word. "I. Can't. Hate My. Brother."

"An accident of birth. Why should I suffer because you're stuck with him for life?" Blue tossed the magazine toward the garbage can next to her desk. *Yes!* Nothing but net. "Do us both a favor and disown the twit."

"Can't. I love him." Staring at the wine as she swirled it around, Jordyn smiled. "Like him, too. Most of the time. Except when he sticks his nose into my love life." Her smile slipped. "At those times, we're in complete agreement. Protective big brother equals massive jackass."

"Do me a favor? Try forgetting the good times and concentrate on the jackassery? Not all the time. Just when I feel like going on a rant."

"Not going to happen." Jordyn sighed with fake sympathy. "Sorry. It's my duty—as your best friend—to call you out when you tilt toward the unreasonable. What happened between you and Spencer is ancient history. You took that job in New York right out of college. Gained some perspective—your words if you remember."

Blue nodded. She spent four years on the other side of the

country. Not exactly self-imposed exile. She graduated with three very tempting job offers on the table. One in San Francisco. One in Chicago. One in New York.

When she made her choice, it just happened to be the city farthest from Seattle. Purely coincidental. Her decision had been based on merit—not a broken heart.

The decision to come back to where she was born—where she grew up and went to college—was made for the same reason. Blue had a chance at her dream job. Spencer had nothing to do with it. She was over him. The past was firmly in her rearview mirror.

Better than that. Sometime over the past years—when she hadn't been paying attention—Blue had turned a corner. When she looked into that mirror, the road was clear for miles. No ex-boyfriend-related baggage anywhere to be seen.

Ready to come home, all Blue needed was word that she'd gotten the job. It seemed like a slam dunk—or as close to one as possible when she threw in the human element. She was qualified—extremely so.

Assistant to the head of public relations for the Seattle Cyclones. In two years, when head PR man Vance Sutter retired, his job would be hers for the taking.

The interview had gone better than she could have hoped. When she walked out, there were smiles all around.

Certain she was a shoe-in, Blue had boarded the return flight to

New York already anticipating making the trip again. One way west. This time to stay. For good.

Unfortunately, instead of smooth, clear water, there would be some choppy waves ahead. It began with a rumor that floated Blue's way a few days later.

Instead of hiring her, the Cyclones would promote from within.

The team had the right to choose who they wanted. But Blue felt there had to be more to it. If management had a problem with her, she wanted to know why.

"The decision is still under debate, Blue."

"Two days ago, you practically assured me the job was mine. What could have changed in forty-eight hours?"

Everett Peale had nothing to do with who the Cyclones hired or fired. His job was in the accounting department. Strictly middle management. But he'd known Blue since she was a little girl. He and her father had been friends since high school.

She couldn't count the number of Sundays the three of them had spent at the ballpark. Loyal to the end, they attended as often as possible. Through the team's good years *and* bad.

Everett's job with the Cyclones meant they could get great seats at a great price. Often, they didn't pay a dime. If it had been up to Blue, she'd have lived at the ballpark.

Baseball was her first true love. And unlike a certain man she once thought she knew better than herself, the game had never let her down. On occasion, it could break her heart. But by the next day—or the beginning of the next Spring Training—she'd moved on. Ready to forgive and forget.

When it came to baseball, hope always sprang eternal.

"I've heard some talk. But at this point, it's nothing but rumors," Everett hastened to inform Blue. "Take it with a grain of salt. Chances are, it's just people talking. Nothing more."

"Talking about what?"

"I didn't want to tell you. If you end up getting the job, what would be the point? Right?"

"Everett…"

Blue loved the man to death. He was like a second father. However, at times, extracting information was harder than pulling wisdom teeth. Since she had hers removed when she was seventeen, she was confident with the comparison.

"I hope I don't regret telling you this." Everett let out a hefty sigh. "I heard somebody is trying to block the team from hiring you."

"Somebody?"

"I can't verify what I heard. Secondhand… No. More like fourth-hand information." When Blue let out a frustrated growl, Everett relented. "Spencer Kraig. There. Are you happy?"

Blue's legs had given out, grateful she was in her office at work. Alone. Where nobody could see what she imagined was her face drained of any color.

"Why would Spencer care one way or the other?"

Even as Blue asked the question, she pictured her last meeting with Spencer Kraig. They hadn't parted on the best of terms—to put it mildly. But that was over four years ago. And she'd been the one with the trampled-on heart. The one who had been wronged.

If Spencer used his clout as the team's star player to keep Blue from getting the job with the Cyclones, his reason was a mystery. She'd called him a lot of names. Arrogant. Self-involved. Heartless. But she'd never thought of him as spiteful. Yet, what other motive could there be?

"It's early days," Everett tried to assure her. "Stay positive."

"I'll try. Promise you won't mention any of this to my father." Spencer—no matter how much he helped the Cyclones—was still in Clark O'Hara's dog house. She saw no reason to stir up old feelings.

"I won't. You deserve this job. It's what you've dreamed about for most of your life. I believe that in the end, management will do the right thing."

Blue hadn't been so certain. She knew that right was the last thing an employer thought about. Their motivation always came down to the bottom line. To make money, they needed bodies in the seats.

Spencer was a big reason the Cyclones had played in front of a packed stadium for the past three years.

The team's first priority was keeping their superstar third baseman happy. If Spencer made it clear that hiring Blue would turn his smile upside down, she could kiss her dream goodbye.

A week passed. Then two. Blue's normally robust appetite pretty much evaporated. At night—rather than a sound night's sleep—she tossed and turned. By the third week, she was ready to call the Cyclones and tell them where to stick their job.

Then, with little fanfare—and no warning—Blue received word. The job was hers. The team hadn't explained what had taken so long. And she hadn't asked.

Two months later, Blue was back in Seattle. Happy with the way things had worked out. Yet, her nerves when it came to Spencer were still raw. She didn't know what he'd done—or hadn't done. Chances were good she'd never find out.

Blue wanted to let it go. Really. She did. But every now and then, it crept from the back of her mind. Had Spencer tried to keep her from working for the Cyclones? When he—as much as anybody—knew how much the job meant to her?

Knowing Spencer might be guilty felt like a betrayal. Deep and profound. Though Blue was no longer in love with him. And she hadn't expected them to be friends. She hadn't considered the idea of him being her enemy.

Worse than anger. It hurt Blue's heart.

"You're right," Blue said to Jordyn, pulling her thoughts out of the past. "I don't hate Spencer."

"And you never did," Jordyn said with an optimism that made Blue laugh.

"Sorry. You can't rewrite history. My hatred for Spencer burned in my gut for a long time. Now? Ashes. Nothing more."

"I don't believe that."

One of Jordyn's best qualities—besides her unswerving loyalty and support—was her ability to find hope when the rest of humanity would have given up long ago.

On the outside, her friend had the appearance of a sophisticated, cosmopolitan woman. And that's what Jordyn was. Like her brother, she'd been blessed with excellent genes. From the time she was a young teenager, modeling agencies begged her to sign with them.

But Jordyn wasn't interested. She ran an internationally successful high-end cosmetics company that she started in college with nothing but a few hundred dollars and the will to make it happen. A tough negotiator, she could be ruthless when necessary.

That said, on the inside—when it came to the people she loved—Jordyn was a big, fluffy marshmallow. She wanted Blue to be happy. And despite everything that had happened, she clung to the belief that Spencer was somehow the key.

Blue picked up her wine, saluting her best friend.

"Here's to your need for a happily ever after ending. I hope you find one someday."

Jordyn frowned into her glass. "What about you?"

"Okay. I hope *I* find one. Love would be nice. Great. However, I refuse to be one of those women who constantly laments the lack of a man in her life. Living alone isn't sad, Jordyn. Do you know what is? Not appreciating all the things I have right here. Right now."

"We have it pretty good, don't we?"

Blue nodded. "We've been blessed with good health. Our families were practically pulled from the *Leave it to Beaver* playbook—with more personality. And best of all, we have each other."

Smiling, Jordyn clinked her glass with Blue's.

"I won't stop hoping for love."

"Me neither. However," Blue said with absolute conviction. "If *the one* is out there, his name is *not* Spencer Kraig."

CHAPTER TWO

"ON PAPER, SEATTLE is the team to beat next season. I predict, come October, the Cyclones will be World Series champions. With their pitching and run-producing power, they look almost unbeatable."

Rolling his eyes, Spencer Kraig turned off the television. How many times had some talking head used the term *"on paper"* when making their pre-season predictions? It meant nothing. Proved nothing.

Until the teams hit the field. Until every game was played. Every pitch hurled. Every batter swung for the fences. Until then? Those predictions were worth about as much as the paper on which they were printed.

Or in this case, the airwaves on which they were broadcast.

"Did we ever buy into the hype?" Nick Sanders asked, burrowing through Spencer's refrigerator.

"Probably." From the other side of the room, Travis Forsythe chimed in his two cents worth, expertly sending a ball toward its target on the vintage pinball machine. "When we were starry-eyed rookies, and we were convinced that once we made it to the big leagues, life would be nothing but champagne and championship rings."

"We have the champagne part." Nick held up a chilled bottle of

Bollinger. "When the hell do we get the rings?"

As he stood looking out at the shores of Lake Washington, Spencer asked himself the same thing. He was pushing thirty. For an athlete, an interesting age. In some sports—football most notably—he'd be heading into the twilight of his career.

Baseball was a different animal. Spencer was in his prime. Barring any major injuries, he'd stay there for the next four or five years. He could easily remain productive while pushing forty—or a bit beyond.

All of which was great. Terrific. Spencer loved the game. During the season, it drove his waking hours. Off-season, he spent a major chunk of his time getting his body ready for the next grueling one-hundred-and-sixty-two game campaign. But that didn't change one overriding fact.

Spencer wanted his team to win the World Series.

Three years straight—every year since Spencer signed his free agent contract—the Cyclones had made it to the postseason. Three years running, they came away empty handed.

Some athletes fell into championships during their first year or two. Others toiled a whole career without a sniff at the brass ring. A point came in every baseball player's career—after the money, the fame, the personal glory—when a championship became more and more important.

Spencer was lucky. Unlike some players who knew their team

was flat-out bad, he was part of a talented crew. They had the pitching. The hitting. The speed. Their defense was second to none.

Still, a baseball season was a marathon, not a sprint. Between April and October so much had to go right. At the end of the year, records and stats were thrown out the window. Often, the hottest team going into the playoffs won it all—not the one that looked best '*on paper*.'

Turning, Spencer looked at his teammates—his friends.

"When do we get the rings?" he asked. "Do you want a cliché or do you want the truth?"

Travis joined Nick by the refrigerator, pushing his friend out of the way. Grabbing a beer, he twisted off the cap.

"I live for clichés," he said, eyes twinkling as he took a sip. "Hell, today I have on my big boy pants. Hit me with the truth, Yoda."

Spencer's nickname hadn't come about because he was old, green, and wrinkled. The Yoda moniker stuck because—even when he was green as grass and playing his first full season—his teammates gravitated toward him for advice.

The wisdom and mentoring came a little later. But they dubbed him Yoda then, and Yoda it would stay.

"We may never get the hardware." Spencer held up his right hand, wiggling the ring finger. When Nick and Travis let out a stream of curse words, he grinned. "Injuries are mother fuckers. How close were we last year? One game away from playing in the Series. Carlos goes down with a pulled hamstring. Rodriguez cuts his finger opening a shitass can of chili."

Nick groaned. "Don't remind me. One night away from pitching the biggest game of his career and he can't get somebody else to fix him a snack?"

"The point is, shit happens. Shit that nobody can predict."

"In other words, play the damn game and play hard. That's all any of us can do."

Spencer didn't mind having his words thrown back at him. Though, technically, they weren't his. They belonged to his first minor league manager. Who heard them from his first manager. And so on.

One of the many reasons Spencer loved baseball so much was the tradition. More than any other sport he knew, this one thrived on the tried and true.

In a world filled with uncertainty and turmoil, he found something comforting in knowing baseball—and its clichés—was a constant he could count on not to change.

"It's December and ESPN has already handed us the championship. I'm going to bask. At least for today."

Grinning at Nick, Travis finished off his beer. "I know what that means. Which of your bevy of beauties will you choose to help you bask?"

"I have yet to pare down the list." Nick took out his phone. "Feels like a smorgasbord type of night. Ten? Maybe twelve? A few shots of Kentucky's finest should help me narrow the field. Who's with me?"

"Sure." Travis grabbed his jacket. "Tonight we bask. Tomorrow, it's back to the weight room. I need to put on another five or six pounds of muscle before Spring Training." As if holding a bat, he made a sweeping swing. Known as the league's premier defensive shortstop, this year Travis planned on upping his power numbers. "Mark me down for forty homers."

"How about it, Spence? You up for some female companionship?"

Not so very long ago, Spencer wouldn't have hesitated. He used to love a good time out with friends—the more beautiful women, the better. That hadn't changed. Exactly. Was it his fault that a certain redhead entered his thoughts more and more these days? At some damn inconvenient moments?

When a man was having sex with one woman, he shouldn't see another's face. Or remember the feel of her lips. Or swear that her one-and-only scent had entered the room, swirling around him, intoxicating his senses.

Spencer was annoyed by the intrusion. But he shouldn't be surprised. Blue O'Hara was an original. Always had been. As a little girl, she'd been impossible to ignore with her shock of bright red hair and expressive gray eyes.

As Blue grew older, she dazzled in a different way. Seemingly overnight, she transformed from precocious and cute to a beautiful, desirable woman. Asking Spencer to resist her charms would have been like asking a lion to ignore a lamb, tethered and welcoming.

The attraction was mutual. The affair had been intensely passionate. When it ended, the blame was all Spencer's. He hadn't been ready for anything serious. Dumping Blue—he wished he could think of a nicer way to say it—hadn't been easy. As arrogant as it sounded, he knew it had been the right decision. For both of them.

Other than the occasional twinge—usually when he spotted a flash of red hair in a crowded room—Spencer rarely thought about Blue. She lived on the other side of the country. She had her own life. She was doing just fine—according to his sister.

Four years Blue free. They hadn't seen each other or communicated in any way. Yet the second she moved back to Seattle, somehow, her spirit haunted him, reminding him of how they once were together.

Spencer rubbed the back of his neck, trying to loosen the suddenly tense muscles. They ended a long time ago. And that was how he wanted it to stay.

"I don't want her back," Spencer muttered.

"What was that?" Nick asked, car keys in hand. "Something about a woman's back?"

"That spot right at the base?" Travis made a humming sound. "So soft and warm. Damn." With more force than necessary, he shoved an arm into the sleeve of his jacket. "I've been spending too much time with you guys. Let's get going."

Following Travis, Nick sent an inquiring look over his shoulder. "What about it? You coming?"

Tired of himself—and his musings—Spencer nodded.

"What the hell. We're only young once."

Young. Free. With every intention of staying that way.

CHAPTER THREE

THE RESTAURANT WAS lit with the point of creating a warm, elegant, intimate setting.

Candles graced every table, casting a romantic glow onto the sparkling silver, the pristine white china and—most important— the faces of the diners. From the view of Puget Sound to the background music—Rachmaninoff played by the softest of violins. The setting perfectly promoted romance.

Blue smiled at her date. There were hundreds, maybe thousands, of women who would appreciate sitting across from a handsome man in such a setting. Unfortunately, she wasn't one of them.

Blind dates were problematic. They began with a great deal of anticipation. Sometimes good. Sometimes bad. Often the results turned out to be somewhere in between.

In Blue's case, she was here under duress—the pressure applied firmly by her mother.

The phone call came just as Blue was leaving for work. She had a meeting at nine-thirty and didn't want to be late. If she hadn't been rushed, she might have gently argued her mother out of the idea.

Or not. Dorothy O'Hara had a will of iron—especially when it came to her children. She considered it her duty to make certain each was happily settled in a relationship. To give the woman credit, she didn't push for marriage. At least not in the first year.

After that—if things were progressing to everybody's satisfaction—all bets were off. Wedding bells were in the not-so-distant future.

So far, Dorothy was one for three in her efforts to watch her children travel through life two by two. In baseball, she would sport a stellar three hundred average. Mom being Mom, she wouldn't be happy until she batted a thousand.

Blue almost didn't answer when she heard the ringtone. She loved her mother. Deeply. Most of the time, she was one of Blue's all-time favorite people. However, at the last two Sunday dinners—surrounded by Blue's snickering siblings—Dorothy had begun to hint—quite loudly—that she knew the nicest young man. He and Blue had so much in common.

When Blue tried to evade the subject, her mother countered at every turn. She could hear her now.

You've been back in Seattle for over a month. It's time to start socializing. It's one dinner. What can it hurt? I've told Warren all about you. He can't wait for Saturday night.

As Blue finished getting ready for her date, she wondered just how anxious Warren Miller really was. Had his mother pushed him to agree? Had he—like Blue—agreed because to do otherwise would mean more pressure, not less?

What an encouraging thought. Blue selected a pair of sparkling hoop earrings from her jewelry case. They looked good with the simple teal-colored dress, her hair fashioned into a low ponytail at the base of her neck. If Warren had the same feelings of trepidation, it didn't bode well for the success of the evening.

On the other hand, perhaps they'd share a laugh over the whole thing and have a wonderful time.

Now that Blue was in the restaurant, sitting opposite Warren, that tiny glimmer of optimism faded with each sip of her overpriced wine.

It seemed that handsome, accomplished, well-heeled attorney Warren Miller had no sense of humor. Or if he did, he hid it under his fake tan and startlingly bright chemically enhanced toothsome smile.

Blue liked to think she was an open-minded person. First impressions were important. But so were second chances. So, she waited patiently through the appetizer as Warren went on and on about himself. She tried to interject a few words as she sampled the excellent main course of beef tenderloin in a light mushroom sauce.

As Warren ordered dessert—without consulting Blue—her viewpoint swerved from hopeful to philosophical. The food was excellent. Her dining companion? Not so much. However, if all she could complain about was a bit of boring dialogue, she could live with that. One night out of her life—to make her mother happy. Hardly the end of the world.

"How about Tuesday night?"

"Excuse me?" Blue asked when she realized that while her mind wandered, Warren continued his monologue. "I'm sorry. What about Tuesday night?"

"The art exhibit that opened downtown? Would you like to go before or after we eat?"

Another date? *Well, crap.* So much for hoping she and Warren were on the same page about how this evening was playing out. Blue wanted it to end as soon as possible. Warren wanted a second helping.

For her mother's sake, Blue could endure an evening of one-sided, mind-numbing conversation. Two? Nope. No way. Not going to happen. Sorry, Mom. Nice try, but this time, you picked a dud.

"I'm flattered, Warren. But—"

"Is that who I think it is?"

Warren's gaze moved across the room. Apparently, she couldn't hold his interest long enough to politely inform him that not only did she not want to go out with him on Tuesday. This would be their last date. Period.

Like a three-year-old with a microsecond attention span, something bigger and brighter had caught Warren's eye.

On a scale of one to ten, Blue wondered if making an excuse that allowed her to slip away before dessert arrived fell on the high or low end of rude behavior. She supposed it depended on who made the call.

As the waitress returned, Blue thanked her, asking that she bring the check right away. With a smile and an understanding nod, the woman produced the already tallied bill.

The bad date club. Every woman was a member, binding them into a universal sisterhood. No need for explanations. They had all been there at one time or another.

Blue took a bite of tiramisu. Enjoyed a sip or two of coffee. Warren was too busy rubbernecking the possible celebrity across the room to touch his. That settled it. Time to thank her date, shake his hand, and call it an evening. At least she had the foresight to drive herself to the restaurant.

"It is!" Warren whispered excitedly. "Can you believe my luck? I can't wait to tell my buddies that I had dinner at the same restaurant as Spencer Kraig."

Spencer? Here? Blue almost whipped her head around to verify Warren's claim. Or, she could drop her face into her hands. Crawl under the table. Find the nearest exit. Run for the hills.

She wasn't ready to meet him. Wasn't mentally prepared—if such a thing were possible. Meeting Spencer was a given. Eventually. Blue had hoped—foolishly—that the time and place would be of her choosing.

"Are you a baseball fan?" Warren asked Blue without moving his gaze from the spot over her shoulder. "Spencer Kraig plays third base for the Cyclones. That's Seattle's team."

Already on edge, Blue wanted to reach across the table and slap Warren upside the head. Instead, reminded him—through gritted teeth—what she did for a living.

"I work in PR. *For* the Cyclones." *You narcissistic idiot.*

Warren wasn't listening. Surprise, surprise

"Oh, my God." Warren straightened his shoulders, fiddling with his already perfect tie. "He's coming this way."

Great. Just freaking great. Blue's shoulders drooped. She wouldn't be on this date—in this restaurant—if she weren't such a good daughter. That fact alone should have given her a pass for at least one night. Let Spencer walk by without stopping. *Please.*

"I thought I recognized you."

That voice. After all this time, it still had a way of sending chills of recognition up her spine.

Bracing herself, Blue turned, raising her gaze. Green eyes, bright as emeralds, met hers.

"Hello, Spencer."

"Hello, Blue."

To say Spencer looked good would be the understatement of this or any other century. Tall. Fit. He wore a dark-blue suit, crisp white shirt, and perfectly polished Italian leather shoes. Expensive and tailored to a T. She remembered well that Spencer had a thing for having his clothing and footwear custom made.

When Blue dated him, his walk-in closet had been filled with row after row, shelf after shelf, of more items than he could possibly wear in one lifetime. She'd teased him. He'd grinned, shrugging it off.

It's one of my few vices, he'd said. Taking Blue into his arms, he whispered in her ear. *Clothes. And incredibly sexy redheads.*

Memories were dangerous things, Blue decided, biting the inside of her cheek to stop herself from letting out a breathy sigh. Damn the memories. And damn Spencer Kraig. It didn't matter that Blue had seen him on television just the other day. Experiencing him in person—especially after four years—was a whole different level of awareness.

"This is a surprise."

Inside, Blue was a mess. Yet her voice sounded calm and casual. Pleased, she gave herself an imaginary pat on the back.

The smile on Spencer's lips was warm. Friendly. The woman on his arm radiated neither. Beautiful. Blue would give her that. But the blonde's expression held as much heat as Alaska in mid-January.

"You know Spencer Kraig?" Warren managed to tear his gaze from Spencer long enough to glance Blue's way. "Why didn't you say anything?"

"Gee, I don't know. I guess it slipped my mind."

The sarcasm dripping off each word went right over Warren's head. But not Spencer's. For a brief second, his eyes met Blue's and the years fell away. Perfectly in tune, there had been a time when they communicated with just a look. The memory made her throat ache. And her spine stiffen.

Regret was inevitable. But it went down a lot easier chased with anger rather than sadness.

"Are you coming or going?" Blue asked, hinting for Spencer to move it along one way or the other.

"We just finished," Spencer countered, knowing exactly what Blue meant. "I'm sorry. Where are my manners? Let me introduce you to my date. Blue O'Hara. Janelle."

"I'm a model," Janelle said, apparently feeling the need to explain her one name moniker.

Warren jumped to his feet, grabbing Spencer's hand, pumping it in a firm manly manner. "Warren Miller. It's a pleasure. I have season tickets."

Nobody was as smooth as Spencer when it came to handling enthusiastic fans. Blue used to marvel at his patience. However, his seemingly endless good cheer did have its limits. There were lines that couldn't be crossed.

The biggest no-no? Don't put Spencer's livelihood in danger.

Warren had an iron grip on Spencer's hand—the one used to scoop up ground balls. Make dazzling defensive plays. Grip the bat. Crushed fingers meant he could do none of those things.

Recognizing the glint of steel in Spencer's green eyes, Blue knew if Warren didn't let go, things could turn very nasty, very fast. Luckily, Janelle—tired of not being the center of attention—unwittingly solved the problem.

"Spencer. Darling. You promised to take me dancing so I can work off that huge dinner."

Huge dinner, my ass. Who was Janelle trying to kid, Blue wondered. Observing the way the waif-thin model clung to Spencer's arm as if in need of support, one had difficulty believing the woman had eaten anything substantial since before the turn of the last century.

Yes, the catty thought wasn't up to Blue's usual standards. Unfair. Even harsh. The kind of remark she normally frowned upon. But, damn it, she was only human. Meeting the one-time love of her life for the first time in ages was stressful business. Since she didn't speak the words, keeping them strictly to herself, she decided to give herself a pass. This time.

Crisis averted, Spencer took back his hand. He nodded toward Warren, turning his attention to Blue.

"I enjoyed seeing you again. We'll talk. Soon."

Was that supposed to be a promise or a threat? Or a threatening promise. Or, had she read way too much into Spencer's words? At this point, Blue had no idea.

Trying to sort out her jumbled thoughts would be an exercise in futility. A good night's sleep and a little perspective. That's what Blue needed.

"We're finished. Why don't we walk out with you?"

Spencer raised an eyebrow, but simply motioned for them to proceed. "After you."

Blue wasn't embarrassed. Warren—the way he chose to act— had nothing to do with her. Happy at the thought of leaving, she slipped on her jacket, picked up her purse, and weaved her way through the restaurant toward the exit.

"You're going dancing?" Blue heard Warren ask as she handed the valet the stub of paper identifying her car. Knowing what was coming, she rolled her eyes. "We'd love to join you."

Oh, no we wouldn't. Blue wanted to wash her face. Brush her teeth. And get into her own bed. Alone. A.S.A.P.

"If Spencer and Janelle don't mind, you go ahead. I have work in the morning."

"One dance. Or two. Then I'll go home with you."

Warren said it like the promise of his company was a treat Blue couldn't resist. Dangle his awesomeness in front of her and watch her jump to do his bidding. Just the thought made her want to laugh. The restraining hand on her arm stirred a more violent response.

"Walk away, Warren."

"But—"

"You heard the lady." Spencer stepped forward, shoulders squared, eyes narrowed. "Walk away."

"I—"

Spencer lowered his voice, sending a warning shiver through Blue's body. "If you want to keep the hand, drop it. Now."

"Go home, Warren." Blue stepped between the two men. In the way of an apology, she smiled at Janelle. "Spencer. May I speak with you? Privately?"

"Sure."

Sending Warren another look of warning, Spencer followed Blue. She stopped a few yards away from their dates, the valet, and several diners who had hovered, anticipating, probably hoping, for a show.

They were in public. Which was precisely the problem.

"Where did you pick up idiot boy?"

"If you remember, I didn't have to pick you up."

Always sharp on the uptake, Spencer immediately caught her meaning.

"Funny," he said, tipping his imaginary hat. "However, I'm talking about tonight."

"Warren isn't the issue. You are." Keeping her voice down,

Blue said a silent thank you to high heels. The added four inches to her height meant she only had to angle her chin a bit to look him directly in the eyes.

"I was raised to help a lady in need."

"I didn't ask for or need your help."

Spencer smiled, thinking to lay on the charm. "Blue—"

"What if Warren had argued? Or worse, taken a swing at you?"

"He'd be on his ass, questioning his sanity."

Blue took a deep, calming breath. "And five minutes later, the video would be on YouTube. An hour later, TMZ would have it."

Spencer shrugged. "So?"

Shaking her head, Blue sighed. "You're right. It wouldn't make the slightest ding on your reputation. The added publicity would probably get another endorsement. But how do you think it would look for the Cyclones' new PR assistant to find herself in the middle of a fight involving one of the team's biggest players?"

"*One* of their biggest players?"

"Arrogant—" Blue turned to stalk off, changing her mind, she hissed. "Was that your plan? To get me in trouble with the front office?"

"Don't be ridiculous. Why would I do that?"

"I know you didn't want me to get the job with the Cyclones. But now that I have it, getting rid of me won't be that easy."

This time when Blue turned on her heel, she kept going.

"What the hell are you talking about?" Spencer hurried after her. "Blue?"

"Have a nice evening, Janelle," Blue waved at the baffled-looking model.

Blue didn't bother to acknowledge Warren who stood next to Janelle, mouth agape. As for Spencer? He could go to hell.

Thanking the valet with a smile and a tip, Blue slid into her car. Inside, her heart raced. She suppressed the urge to hit the gas, shove the pedal to the floor, and burn rubber out of the parking lot.

If she were a different kind of person—reckless instead of sensible—she might have given into the temptation that made her want to drive fast. Or worse, grab Spencer in front of anybody who cared to watch. And kiss him. Really giving him something to think about.

Not so long ago, Blue would have done exactly that. The kiss part at least. A time when she felt free to show the world how she felt about Spencer Kraig.

Reaching the hill that led to her apartment, Blue shifted the car into a lower gear. Traffic was sparse, giving her mind a chance to wander. Naturally, it wandered to thoughts of Spencer.

In the scheme of things, four years seemed like a small amount of time. Yet, somehow, it felt like a lifetime.

The first time Blue imagined kissing Spencer, she was fifteen years old. A silly thought—a whim—that came as quickly as it went. She hadn't spent her teenage years yearning for her best friend's older brother.

Another five years would pass before the thought crossed her mind again.

One kiss. That was all it took for Blue's world to change forever.

CHAPTER FOUR

SIX YEARS EARLIER

"SPENCER IS COMING home tomorrow."

Jordyn made the announcement in a reverential tone—one she'd never used when speaking about her brother.

Blue kept her nose in her sociology book, reaching for a handful of popcorn from the bowl on her desk.

"Big deal. Doesn't he always come home for Christmas?"

"But this is the first time since he was named league MVP."

Something to brag about at any age, Spencer had just turned twenty-four. That made the accomplishment even more impressive. However, Blue couldn't resist ribbing the justifiably proud sister.

"Be still my heart."

"Come on. You're as excited about it as I am. How many MVPs can you say you've personally met? Let alone sat next to at the dinner table."

"I don't know. Give me a minute to think."

A pillow sailed through the air, hitting Blue squarely in the back of the head.

"Nice shot. Tell me again why you gave up your dream to be the first woman to pitch in the majors?"

"Not enough velocity," Jordyn lamented, rubbing her shoulder as if remembering the way it felt after a game. "I was good, though, wasn't I?"

"Best slider I've ever seen. You had those little league runts shaking in their cleats."

"Mm." With a sigh, Jordyn shook off the memory. "I had my glory days. This is Spencer's time."

"You struck out big brother once or twice if you recall."

"As I remind him whenever his britches get too big." Grabbing the bowl of popcorn, Jordyn sat cross-legged on Blue's bed, flipping her long, dark hair over one shoulder. "Thankfully, that isn't as often as it used to be. It's weird. The more national recognition Spencer receives, the more humble he becomes."

"Spencer Kraig? Humble? Are we talking about the same person?"

Blue had known Spencer most of her life. When she and Jordyn met in the first grade, they became instant friends. After that, they practically lived in each other's pockets. If they weren't at one house, they were at the other. As a result, they inherited a second family.

Like Blue's own brother, on occasion, Spencer could be annoying. A royal pain in her backside. However, when push came to shove, she would defend him to her last breath. No questions asked. Because that's what family did.

"Spencer has changed." When Blue snorted, Jordyn shrugged. "You will just have to see for yourself. Dinner tomorrow night."

"I have a date with the library."

Though they were on Christmas break from the University of Washington, Blue wanted to get a jump on next semester's classes.

Blue smiled, thinking of a certain assistant librarian who could always find time during his break for a little necking behind the Greek classics section. Another reason she loved higher education. In the two years since enrolling, her mental prowess had improved greatly.

As for her love life? Blue wouldn't call herself an expert by any means. And sometimes she wondered if the things she did—and the men she did them with—were a bit vanilla. Still, she liked sex. Fun—for the most—she found nothing major to complain about.

Jordyn—well aware of why Blue spent so many nights "*studying*"—dismissed the excuse with a flick of her hand.

"Forget Boring Bruno. Mom is making her manicotti."

Closing her eyes, Blue swore she could smell the spicy tomato sauce, saliva pooling in her mouth. She loved Jordyn's mother. She was smart and funny and caring.

However, what won Blue's heart right from the beginning was Connie Kraig's cooking.

"That's not playing fair."

Smiling—knowing she'd won—Jordyn bounced from the bed.

She wrapped her arms around Blue, giving her a quick hug.

"Spencer is bringing the MVP trophy with him."

"Oh, goody. We get the chance to bask in his glory. I can hardly wait." Blue winked, returning Jordyn's hug. "I promise to be suitably impressed."

"No fun in that," Jordyn laughed, grabbing her backpack from the corner of the room where she'd blindly flung it upon her arrival. "My brother *has* changed. But he's still Spencer. If at some point in the evening he backslides, you have my permission to pull out your verbal darts, take aim at his swelling ego, and pop away."

Alone, Blue chuckled. She wasn't immune to the excitement of sharing in Spencer's accomplishments. Truthfully, she looked forward to taking an up-close look at his trophy.

Not that she'd share that bit of information. Her eagerness would only add to Spencer's already oversized ego.

Spencer and Blue had a very nice, friendly yet semi-antagonistic relationship. A dynamic that they both enjoyed. Since he signed with the St. Louis Cardinals, she'd missed taking jabs at Spencer on an almost daily basis. The baseball season was a long one. In a blink, the holiday would pass, the new year would be upon them, and he'd leave for Spring Training.

After that, Blue probably wouldn't see Spencer again until late fall.

As Blue absently tapped her pen on her desk, her smile

widened. The more she thought of skipping the library for a night with the Kraig clan, the more it appealed to her.

Jordyn was right. Blue could see Boring Bruno any time. Spending time with Spencer—getting under his skin for old time's sake—was an opportunity she couldn't pass up.

"ALL I'M SAYING is that Stan Wilkins had a great year."

"You said he was robbed in the MVP voting."

"Did I? No. I think you misheard. Is your hearing going along with your arm, old man?"

Hearing Spencer's laugh brought an answering smile to Blue's lips.

The night was chilly. A misty fog covered the sidewalk, obscuring their feet from view. In other words, a typical Seattle in December.

Dinner had been a raucous, happy affair. Lots of food, laughter, and good-humored teasing. The table was filled with family—Blue included. Two older siblings—Rick and Reid—plus their spouses. Each had a toddler near the same age who had been lovingly tucked away by Grandma and Grandpa, sleeping soundly, in the spare bedroom.

In deference to Spencer's parents, Blue kept her jabs at a minimum. They were so proud—practically bursting with it—that she didn't want to do anything to put a damper on the evening.

However, now that they were alone, all bets were off.

Spencer had insisted on walking Blue home. She tried to argue—her parents' house was only three blocks away. She couldn't persuade him. Not that she was surprised. The Kraig men took a woman's well-being seriously. If Spencer weren't home, one of them would have accompanied her—even if she only lived across the street.

Taking their time, they strolled along the sidewalk. And the banter began.

"My arm is just fine, Bluebell."

Blue frowned when Spencer used the nickname he'd given her shortly after their first meeting. She hadn't liked it then, and that hadn't changed. A fact of which he was well aware.

"If you need proof, I'll be happy to turn you over my knee and tan your backside."

"Save the kinky stuff for your stable of supermodels. Honestly, Spencer. What would your mother say if she knew you were into that kind of stuff?"

"Blue..." Spencer trailed off with an unmistakable warning in his tone.

"Whips? Chains? Nipple clamps?"

"Jesus. What do you know about such things?"

Blue suppressed her smile. "Wouldn't you like to know?"

"Yes, as a matter of fact. I would."

Nothing teasing about that sentence. Spencer sounded gruff. Every inch the big, protective brother. The difference being that Blue would never think of discussing sex toys with her real brother. The very idea made her shudder, revolted at the thought.

"Relax. There are these amazing things called books. They allow me to learn about all kinds of things I've never experienced personally."

"Books, huh?"

"On campus, they house them in a big building called a library. You should stop by someday."

"Right," Spencer nodded, dragging out the word. "The library. I understand you've become quite fond of the classics. And somebody named Bruno."

Blue didn't deny it, more interested in how Spencer found out.

"Who told you?"

"Jordyn."

"No, she didn't."

Her best friend's loyalty was rock solid. Jordyn didn't share Blue's secrets with anybody.

"You're right, she didn't." As they came to the busy cross street, Spencer automatically switched places with Blue on the sidewalk, putting himself between her and the moving traffic. "I heard the two of you before dinner. Whispering and giggling. Some things never change."

"Ears like a bat," Blue muttered under her breath. Naturally, Spencer heard every word.

"Which proves I heard your comment about Stan Wilkins. So, you honestly believe he's a better third baseman?"

Pretending to contemplate the question, Blue put her hand on her chin, rubbing thoughtfully.

"No. I suppose not."

"Did I deserve the MVP award?"

Of course, he did. But she wasn't ready to give in that easily. Front walkway in sight, Blue ran for the safety of her house. She was fast, her legs long. Unfortunately, Spencer had her beat in both categories.

For a brief second—as she reached for the door—Blue thought she would make a clean getaway. Before she could turn the knob, Spencer had her around the waist. She let out a yelp, finding herself pushed into the shadows near the edge of the porch, her back against the smooth siding.

Spencer had his hands on her wrists, pinning one at her side, the other near her head.

"Fine. You're bigger and stronger. So what?"

"Don't forget faster," Spencer said, his warm breath brushing against Blue's cheek. "Admit it. I deserved to be MVP."

Blue licked her lips. Not an intentionally provocative move. Her purpose was to moisten her suddenly dry lips, not draw

Spencer's gaze to her mouth. But when his eyes lowered, she couldn't help herself. Her tongue slowing traced her bottom lip. Corner to corner.

"Blue."

Spencer said her name as if in a daze. As he lowered his head, his intent clear, Blue felt a moment of panic.

"What are you doing?"

Meeting her gaze, Spencer looked as confused as she felt. With a groan, he whispered, "Hell if I know."

A heartbeat later, his lips covered hers.

Blue sank into the pleasure. The taste. The *wonder*. She felt as if a drug had been shot into her veins. Potent beyond words. And instantly addictive.

This isn't a kiss, she thought, hoping it would never end. Not like any she'd experienced.

Kisses were fun. They left her giddy and happy. This reached deep inside, asking for…? Blue had no idea. All she knew was that if Spencer asked—for anything—she'd give it to him without a second's hesitation.

"Blue. Oh, God, Blue."

Breathing hard, Spencer rested his forehead against hers.

"What was that?" Blue asked, dazed.

"I don't know." Spencer made a sound somewhere between a laugh and a groan. "Kind of took me by surprise."

"Join the club."

"Mm." Releasing her wrists, Spencer's hands slid down Blue's arms, cupping her elbows, moving to her waist. "I should—"

"If you dare apologize, I will knock you on your ass."

"If I were stupid enough to be sorry, I wouldn't blame you." Lips close to her ear, he said, "I *should* go. Give you time to think."

"Kiss me again," Blue said, twining her arms around Spencer's neck. "I'll think tomorrow."

CHAPTER FIVE

PRESENT DAY

SPENCER WALKED INTO the main headquarters of the Seattle Cyclones. He removed his jacket, shaking off the accumulated rain. As he took a step toward the bank of elevators, a young woman with a cap of dark hair and a perky smile greeted him.

"Good morning, Mr. Kraig. My name is Ruby. We haven't met. I'm the new receptionist. May I take your jacket? I don't see your name on anybody's list. Who may I call to tell you're on the way up? Crazy cold day, isn't it? Would you like a cup of something hot? Espresso? Cappuccino? Latte?"

Ruby ran on like an over-caffeinated wind-up toy. Fascinated, Spencer considered stopping her. But he found himself wondering how many words she could rattle off without taking a breath.

"Ruby!" a sharp voice called out, silencing Ruby mid-word. "By now, I shouldn't have to remind you. We don't accost people as they enter the building. Or at any other time."

Looking properly chastised, Ruby nodded. "But, Mrs. Birch. This is Spencer Kraig."

Smartly dressed in a forest-green skirt, cream-colored silk blouse, and sensible yet stylish flats, the older woman sighed, shaking her French twist-coifed head.

"I'm well aware, Ruby. Finish typing those letters."."

With a sigh, Ruby did as she was told.

"Hello, Sheila."

"It's good to see you, Spencer." Sheila smiled, giving Spencer's hand a friendly squeeze. "I'm sorry about Ruby. She's new. And young. And enthusiastic."

"Time will take care of the new and young part," Spencer laughed.

"And temper the enthusiasm."

Sheila Birch had worked for the Cyclones longer than Spencer had been alive. Office manager, she ran a tight ship. But at heart, she was a diehard baseball fan *and* the reason she didn't fire Ruby for a little thing like gushing over a superstar athlete. She remembered what it felt like to see her heroes up close for the first time.

Besides, the girl was a good worker. Not an easy quality to find.

"Since when has your enthusiasm been tempered? You cheer as loudly as anybody when the Cyclones win."

"And die a little when they lose. However, those emotions belong at the ballpark. Not the office." Sheila raised her voice, making certain her words reached the front desk and an eavesdropping Ruby.

Over Sheila's head, Spencer sent Ruby a wink. Color flooded the young woman's face as she reached to answer the phone. Flustered, she almost dropped the receiver.

"Was that necessary?" Sheila asked, witness to the effect Spencer had on her receptionist. "Your winks have the power to stop traffic."

Spencer raised an eyebrow at what he considered a major exaggeration. Sheila held her ground.

"You don't see it, but the rest of us do. Look at poor Ruby. She'll be fumbling and stumbling for the rest of the morning all because of you. You've been given a powerful weapon, Yoda. Learn to use it wisely."

The teasing twinkle in Sheila's eyes made Spencer grin. Deliberately, he winked. She merely crossed her arms, her expression unchanged.

"Some of us are naturally immune. Now, enough flirting, young man. Ruby had one thing right. You don't have an appointment with anybody in the building. Not that it matters. Who are you here to see?"

"Norris Grant."

In a snap, Sheila morphed from friend to office manager. Moving to the desk, she picked up the phone. She didn't expect him to give her a reason. Spencer's stature meant she put his request right through. No questions asked.

"Arlene? Spencer Kraig would like to see Mr. Grant." Sheila listened, nodding. "I'll send him right up."

"Thank you, Sheila."

As Spencer approached the elevators, a ding sounded. Doors slid open. He waited for the car to empty before entering. He hit the button for the seventh floor and waited.

Norris Grant was a ruse. Spencer's real reason for being there had nothing to do with the vice president in charge of player development. Not that he let Norris know. He stopped by his friend's office. Gave him the old, *I was just in the neighborhood*, line.

After a few minutes shooting the breeze, Spencer took another elevator ride, this time to the ninth floor and the office of a certain redhead. One Blue O'Hara.

Something Blue said the night before had planted itself in Spencer's brain. A niggling annoyance that he had to clear up before it drove him crazy.

I know you didn't want me to get the job with the Cyclones.

Blue hadn't accused him. She didn't make it a question. Angry. A little hurt. She believed what she said. If he hadn't been so surprised, Spencer would have denied it then and there. But before he could, she was in her car, driving away in what he could only describe as a fit of self-righteous indignation.

The hell with that.

Spencer had done some things he wasn't very proud of—once or twice. But trying to block Blue's career opportunity wasn't one of them. Where she'd gotten the mistaken idea, he couldn't say. But he planned on finding out.

As he approached the reception area, a man in a Cyclones' t-shirt—with hair dyed a matching dark blue with white stripes—greeted him. Unlike Ruby, the man wasn't terribly impressed by the sight of Spencer Kraig.

"May I help you?"

It seemed odd that someone who put that much effort into looking like a walking Cyclones' advertisement didn't recognize one of the team's most visible players. But Spencer didn't really care. At the moment, he had more important things on his mind.

"I'd like to speak to Blue O'Hara."

The man gave Spencer a smile that didn't reach beyond the slight twitch of his lips. He glanced at his computer.

"Do you have an appointment?"

"No. I tell you what, Ernie," Spencer said, reading the name tag pinned just above the swirling C in the Cyclone logo on the man's t-shirt. "If you'd tell Ms. O'Hara that Spencer Kraig is here, I'm sure she'll see me."

Actually, Spencer had no idea how Blue would react. She might let him into her office. Knowing Blue—if she were genuinely pissed off—her first instinct would be to have him thrown from the building. Though causing such a spectacle was hardly an option no matter how tempting she might find it.

Ernie swallowed nervously. He hadn't recognized the face, but Spencer's name rang all kinds of bells.

"Of course, Mr. Kraig. I'm sorry. Just give me a second." Wiping the newly formed beads of sweat from his upper lip, Ernie lifted the phone.

"Hello? Ms. O'Hara? Mr. Spencer Kraig is here in the reception area."

Ernie listened, his mouth dropping open. Swallowing again, he looked at Spencer, his eyes pleading. "Ms. O'Hara would like to speak with you."

Taking pity on the man, Spencer raised the receiver to his ear. "Blue."

"What do you want, Spencer?"

"What I don't want is to stand out here like a leper. Jesus, Blue. I'm ten feet from your office door. Stop acting like a child and let me in."

"Calling me a child in front of my assistant—at my place of business—isn't the way to get what you want."

"You know the old saying about the squeaky wheel, Bluebell."

"Honestly? You sound more like a child than I do." Spencer heard Blue's exasperated sigh. He'd take that over anger any day. "Can we do this in ten minutes or less?"

Spencer almost made a joke. One of a sexual nature. He caught himself, remembering where he was.

"I can't make any guarantees."

"You never could," Blue muttered. "Fine," she said after a brief pause. "Come in."

Spencer handed Ernie the phone.

"Yes, Ms. O'Hara. Your lunch appointment is at twelve-thirty."

Setting down the phone, Ernie rushed around his desk, opening the door for Spencer.

The office wasn't anything special. Small. A little cramped. Four walls without a window. But Blue had added a few personal touches—family pictures in antique frames and a bright blue paperweight made of solid glass—that made the room feel a little more welcoming.

Spencer wished he could say the same for the expression on Blue's face.

"You don't look in the mood for pleasantries."

"No kidding." Blue didn't rise to greet him, staying in her seat, keeping the wooden desk between them. She crossed her arms over her chest and waited.

"At the risk of exceeding my allotted ten-minute window, may I say that you look good, Blue. I should have said so last night. But," Spencer shrugged. "The moment passed."

"Is that why you're here? To rectify your error?"

Unconcerned when Blue didn't ask him to sit, Spencer moved to the chair opposite her. "You were beautiful at twenty-two. Four years later. You're gorgeous. Keep a lid on that redhead's temper. It isn't flattery if I'm stating a fact."

Even in the harsh fluorescent light, Blue's skin glowed like burnished porcelain, a testament to her Irish ancestors. Her figure had always run toward slender, but she'd acquired a few more curves—in all the right places.

And of course, that face.

When Blue was younger, her every emotion would travel across her features, telling a story. Happiness. Anger. Sorrow. And love. Spencer remembered the way her gray eyes glowed the first time she said the words to him.

Right now, those same eyes narrowed. A sure sign of Blue's growing impatience.

"Great. Fine. Wonderful. You want to exchange compliments?" Blue threw up her hands. "I'm freaking gorgeous, and you get more handsome with every passing year."

Lips twitching, Spencer nodded as if accepting his due. His show of arrogance had the desired effect. The gray of Blue's eyes turned a stormy silver.

"You're trying to piss me off," Blue accused.

"Yes."

"Why?"

"Nostalgia?"

Spencer had always enjoyed pushing Blue's buttons. She was quick to anger. And just as quickly, she'd laugh it off. He didn't know which he enjoyed more. The dark flash of her eyes, or the bright curve of her lips.

In the next instant, he had his answer. Blue's smile—even a reluctant one. He couldn't imagine anything better in the world.

Blue sat back in her chair, shaking her head. "Let's start again, shall we? Why are you here, Spencer? Is there something you need from the PR department?"

"My visit is personal."

"I see." No longer relaxed, Blue placed her hands on the desk. "We moved past personal a long time ago, Spencer."

"You're right. Four years is a long time. I'd like for us to be friends."

"I wanted that, too. But…" Blue sighed.

There. She gave Spencer the perfect opening. *But what*?

"What made you think I didn't want you to have this job?"

Blue hesitated. Then, as if making up her mind, she met Spencer's gaze.

"I was told—from a reliable source—that you made your objections clear to the team."

"That isn't true."

"Something delayed their decision. From what I understand, I was the frontrunner. Then I wasn't. Something—or somebody—raised some red flags."

"Whatever happened, I had nothing to do with it. Do you believe me?"

The sadness in Blue's eyes sent a dart toward his heart. At the last second, the projectile swerved, missing by inches, telling Spencer that his word still meant something.

"I don't understand. I had a great interview. When I flew back to New York, I was certain I had the job. If you didn't say something, who did?"

Spencer had no idea. "I received a call from the team president."

"Not an everyday occurrence," Blue said with a frown.

"You're right." Spencer and Eric Bryce weren't exactly casual chat buddies. An unexpected call meant something out of the ordinary was in the wind. "He asked me about you. It isn't common knowledge that we dated. Nor is it a secret. It's more—"

"Ancient history?"

"Let's not age us any more than necessary," Spencer chuckled. "It seems that somebody—Eric didn't name names—whispered in his ear that since your job will require you to travel with the team quite a bit, I might object."

Blue's mouth twisted. "Your sensibilities are important. Mine aren't."

"I have an obscenely large guaranteed contract. You don't."

"Money." Blue's tone was philosophical.

"It gives me a certain amount of clout. Delivering on the field gives me even more. You deserved to get this job, Blue. And I made certain Eric Bryce knew how I felt."

"Thank you, Spencer."

Slowly, Spencer grinned. "I bet you never thought you'd be saying that today."

"Or any other day." Blue returned his smile. And—as always—it made his stomach do a slow roll.

"I'd like to know who tried to sabotage me."

"Does it really matter?" Spencer asked.

"Only if they plan on undermining me in the future." Standing, Blue took her jacket from the back of her chair. "Rather than worry about it, I'll do the best job possible. If anybody has a problem with that, they can go to hell."

"Sounds like a plan." Spencer helped Blue on with her jacket, catching the pleased surprise that flashed across her face.

"Brace yourself for another thank you."

His hands lingered ever so briefly on Blue's shoulders before dropping them to his sides.

"A second thank you in one day? What did I do to deserve that?"

"You made an effort to clear the air between us."

"Either that or drive myself crazy wondering what I'd done."

Blue raised her hand as if she would touch him. To Spencer's disappointment, she changed her mind at the last second.

"Let's try to be friends."

"We're already friends, Blue. We always were." Spencer opened the door moving to the side to let her go first. "All we have to do is remember."

"I did a lot of that last night."

Before she could stop him, Spencer took Blue's hand. "I won't ask you to forget the bad times. Just, maybe, think of the good ones as often as possible."

Firmly, Blue took back her hand. But when she looked at him, her eyes were a clear, bright gray.

"Maybe I will."

CHAPTER SIX

"When is your next date with Wonderful Warren?" Jordyn asked as they took their seats in the movie theater.

"Funny. Ha, freaking, ha." Blue crossed her legs, her booted foot lightly tapping the empty chair in front of her. "The only good thing about that date was my mother's reaction. She was so embarrassed by Warren's behavior I might be safe from the fix-ups. At least in the foreseeable future."

"You found a trace of victory in a bad date. Yay! Do me a favor and send the memo *my* mother's way."

"Enough talk about men—bad or otherwise. Pick a different subject."

"I'm on it. After I say one more man-related thing."

Blue rolled her eyes dramatically. "Fine."

"I'm glad you and Spencer cleared the air. Though I'm not happy that you didn't tell me what happened."

From the moment Blue and Spencer started dating, an awkward no-man's land developed between her and Jordyn. Things she'd have told her best friend were off limits to Spencer's sister.

"In a strictly friendly way," Blue clarified. She didn't want Jordyn to get the wrong idea.

Jordyn raised an eyebrow—a gesture so like Spencer's that Blue wondered why she hadn't noticed it before.

"Right. Just friends." Under her breath, Jordyn added, "For now."

"Jordyn..."

"All I'm saying is some of the best love stories are the ones with second chances."

"Jordyn." Blue's tone went from a warning to something more philosophical. "Spencer was my first love. For two years, I thought we were practically perfect. Then, we weren't."

"Because Spencer broke your heart. But—"

A healed heart carried scars. Sometimes, no matter how much time had passed, those scars tended to ache. Blue closed her eyes, listening. She felt a twinge. However, the beat was strong and steady.

"Spencer broke my heart. Period. No ifs, ands, or buts. As I told him, I want us to be friends. Time will tell if that is possible."

"How is your job going?" Jordyn asked.

Blue smiled. Change of subject complete.

"Good. Borderline great. Vance Sutter is a bit of a curmudgeon. He seems stuck in his ways."

Talk about putting it mildly. Vance wanted things done his way. Which meant the way he'd done them for over twenty years. Blue had all kinds of ideas to bring the public relations department into the twenty-first century. Those ideas were a big part of why she'd been hired.

"I want to give myself a chance to settle in. Do I approach Vance with a straight-to-the-point attitude? Or will it take something subtler."

"He resents that you're a woman."

Jordyn was her own boss. But that didn't mean she was immune to sexism. There would always be men—and other women, unfortunately—who resented a woman's success. Luckily, Blue and Jordyn had grown up with fathers who encouraged them to shine as brightly as their talent and brains allowed.

"Vance doesn't like anybody who has new ideas. My gender doesn't help, but something tells me he wouldn't have welcomed a young, forward-thinking man either."

"Knowing he's slated for the ax can't help."

Blue frowned. "I was told retirement is Vance's choice. Now that I've met him, I'm not so sure."

"You have nothing to do with the decision, Blue. In two years, you'll be head of PR for the Cyclones."

"If I show them I can do it." Mentally, Blue crossed her fingers. "That is the plan."

If management kept their word. Nothing was in writing. And a lot could happen in two years.

"When have you ever failed to get something you really put your mind to?"

"Never."

"There you go." Jordyn lowered her voice as the lights dimmed. "By the time we hit thirty, we'll rule the Seattle business scene. You on the sports side, me on the entrepreneurial side.

Blue had lost track of the times they shared their dreams of making it to the top. On their own. No helping hands. The exact details would vary. When she was fourteen, Blue didn't know she'd choose public relations. Jordyn hadn't decided on selling high-end beauty products in five stores and counting.

However, they were confident—that no matter their paths— they couldn't fail.

"We rock," Blue said.

Jordyn bumped her fist to Blue's.

"Damn straight, we do."

"WE HAVE THREE players scheduled to appear on the *Today Show* next week."

Vance Sutter continued to study his computer screen as he spoke to Blue. They had fallen into an increasingly annoying routine during their morning meetings. He did all the talking. Her one contribution? Listen. In silence.

Blue's opinions weren't welcome. She was allowed to speak but only if she kept her responses to certain phrases. *Yes, Vance. Whatever you say, Vance. You're a PR god, Vance.*

Okay. That might be a bit of an exaggeration. But not much.

After two months, the routine was getting old.

Blue had racked her brain trying to figure out the best way to get around Vance's prejudice toward her. Was it her gender? Her age? Or the fact that she—or anybody who had her job—reminded him that his time with the Cyclones had a finish line.

Whatever Vance's problem, he was making it difficult for Blue. Was that the idea? Force her to quit out of frustration. Or give management no option but to fire her because she wasn't pulling her weight.

A task rendered impossible when she was given so little to do. Vance had her doing what amounted to gopher work.

Vance hadn't the nerve to ask Blue to get him coffee. Perhaps he had a line he wouldn't cross. Or maybe he was just waiting for the right moment, hoping it would be the proverbial straw. The hell with the camel.

What Vance didn't know was that Blue didn't break. She refused to live her life as a passive observer. Even worse, a victim of a middle-aged man's vindictiveness.

Frustrated, Blue listened as Vance droned on. She'd bide her time. For now. If she didn't make a breakthrough, she'd have no recourse but to go over her boss' head.

Blue knew just the shoes she'd wear. Red patent-leather pumps. The spiked five-inch heels would leave some nice gouges along Vance's rapidly receding hairline.

"Are you listening?"

"Of course, Vance. I'm hanging on your every word."

Vance's eyes narrowed as if trying to decide if Blue's words were serious or sarcastic. When she met his gaze—clear and direct—he snorted, letting the moment pass without comment.

"I need you to go to New York to be with the players during their *Today Show* appearance. Keep close tabs. It's morning television. Moms. Grandmas and Grandpas. Little kids. Make certain our guys don't say anything out of line."

"How am I supposed to do that?"

"Figure it out. You're supposed to be good at your job. I can't hold your hand from three thousand miles away."

As Vance opened the bottom drawer of his desk, his head no longer in her line of sight, Blue realized he considered the subject closed. She did not.

"These are three grown men. Veteran players who between them have been in the league for close to three decades. Do you honestly expect me to treat them like children?"

"I expect you to do the job I've assigned you. Unless you think you aren't up to it."

"It isn't a job, Vance," Blue said, proud of herself for holding her temper. "It's busy work."

"I don't agree." Vance's smirk said otherwise. "Watts, Hernandez, and Peterson will be in New York to attend a MLB charity event. Which means they're representatives of the Cyclones. We don't want them embarrassing the franchise, do we?"

Blue's smartest move would be to nod and carry out the bogus assignment. But she couldn't help herself. The snarky comment just slipped out.

"Should I bring along a ruler to slap their knuckles if they get out of line?"

Vance shut the drawer with a snap, his ruddy complexion mottled with color.

"Is that supposed to be a joke? Or are you questioning my authority?"

"A joke. For which I apologize." Blue sighed. She didn't want her work environment to be toxic. "We haven't gotten off to a great start, Vance. Can we try again? A reset—so to speak."

"Is there a problem? I'm not aware of it."

Vance's overly dramatic look of surprise would have been comical in any other situation. Blue felt a wave of regret followed by a slow-burning anger. She'd hoped that Vance would treat her as a protégé.

Because at heart, they shared a love for the game.

Though their styles differed greatly—old school vs. new—Blue believed they could co-exist. Even thrive. The way baseball thrived while embracing its storied traditions.

It seemed Vance didn't agree.

"Do your job, Miss O'Hara. That's *all* I ask."

In other words, forget a friendly working environment.

Blue couldn't accept she had no other option. For the most part, she liked people. And they liked her. She wasn't ready to give up quite yet. But it felt like Vance might turn out to be the exception.

With a nod, Blue left the office. It looked like she was on her way back to New York. A lot sooner than expected.

THERE WERE MANY great things about Seattle.

The music and food scenes were right up there with any city in the world. Activities to match anybody's interests. Mountains to climb. Waterways to explore. Islands on one side. A rainforest on the other. And so much in between. Despite its reputation, the weather—in the summer—was filled with temperate, sunny days.

Spencer loved this city. He was born here. Raised here. He grew up a devoted Cyclones fan with the dream of one day wearing their uniform. Signing with the team as a free agent was one of the proudest days of his life.

Baseball? Played in his hometown? In front of friends and family?

The reality—Spencer was happy to say—had far exceeded all expectations.

With all Seattle had to offer, the best part for Spencer had to be the time he found to spend with his family. Since he left for college, that hadn't been possible on a regular basis.

Now that Spencer was back—for good, he hoped—he could see them as often as he liked.

The Kraig clan was a tight-knit group. Spencer had a childhood that on the surface, seemed to be ripped from a Norman Rockwell painting. Probe a little deeper, and boom! More Rockwell.

They were the real deal. Normal through and through—whatever that meant. They had dinner together almost every night. Took long, memorable summer vacations. Holidays and birthdays were celebrated with equal parts love, reverence, and exuberance.

Still, as much as Spencer had missed them, he knew that the time away had been good for him. Some might say vitally important. He had forged his own life. Established his independence. If he'd stayed in Seattle to play college ball. If the Cyclones had drafted him instead of St. Louis. Spencer wouldn't be the same man.

Not bad, per se. Just… different.

Besides giving him a better sense of himself, the time away gifted Spencer with a new appreciation of the people closest to him. After watching and listening to other players, he learned that Dorothy and Byron Kraig weren't the average parents.

Not once had they pushed Spencer to play baseball. They didn't ride on the coattails of his success, or expect some kind of reward just for giving him life.

Absolute love and support. Those were the gifts Spencer's parents gave to him. The gifts they gave all four of their children.

Spencer liked nothing better than when the family got together for one of Dorothy's epic meals. The food was plentiful. Mouthwatering. And most of all, made with love.

"Stop hogging the potatoes, Rick," Reid complained, jabbing his brother in the ribs.

"Give me the rolls, I'll give you the potatoes."

"Deal."

The routine was tried and true. One Spencer's brothers had played out as long as he could remember. A year separated Rick and Reid. To look at them, he wasn't surprised that they were often mistaken for twins.

While Spencer and Jordyn had dark hair and green eyes—like their father—the oldest Kraig children had been gifted with sandy blond hair, their irises a light brown. Tall. Lanky. They inherited their looks from their mother's side of the family.

The brothers worked with their father in the family business. Kraig's Hardware. Started from scratch when he was eighteen, Byron had turned one small store into ten. With the help of his sons, they expanded to cover all of Washington, Idaho, and Oregon. Plans were in the works to go national.

"Honestly," Dorothy shook her head as Rick and Reid squabbled like children instead of married men with growing families. "Do I need to separate you two?"

Spencer snorted at the chastisement, earning him a warning look.

"Sorry, Mom. Other than the welcome additions of Milly, Evelyn, and the kids, it seems like time stood still while I was gone." Spencer took Dorothy's hand, giving it a warm squeeze. "You and Dad never age. What's your secret?"

Pleased, Dorothy looked around the table. "This. Your brothers and sister. You. Wonderful daughters-in-law. Grandchildren to dote on. Plus, my volunteer work. It keeps me young."

"You look more like our sister than our mother."

"Don't be silly." Dorothy shooed away the idea, but Spencer's words put a flush of color on her cheeks. Patting his hand, she turned to Jordyn. "What were you saying before Rick and Reid's shenanigans interrupted?"

"I spoke with Blue before I left to come over. That jerk Vance Sutter is giving her a hard time."

"What did she say exactly?" Byron Kraig asked, frowning. Blue was part of the family. Hearing she might be having problems set off his fatherly instincts.

"This and that. You know Blue. She won't throw her boss under the bus. But I can tell she's frustrated. It's obvious from his attitude that Sutter is the one who tried to block the Cyclones from hiring her."

"Blue will find a way to make it work. She has a talent for winning people over," Dorothy said with absolute certainty. "But it might not hurt for you to say something to management."

"I could do that," Spencer nodded thoughtfully as if seriously considering his mother's suggestion. "If I wanted Blue to rip me a new one."

"Wouldn't be the first time." Snickering, Rick speared another slice of pot roast from the serving plate. "Seems to me Blue owes you an ass whooping. Or two. Stick your nose in her business, Superstar. When she finds out, give me a call. I want a front row seat for the fireworks."

"Me too." Reid's grin was a bit too anticipatory for Spencer's liking. "Hell, I'll sell tickets. Might as well make a few bucks off little brother's humiliation."

"Little brother will gladly whip your ass."

"You can try."

Said in good fun, Byron chuckled over their antics. Dorothy sighed, her lips twitching. Having her family all together made her heart light. The sounds of gentle, affectionate bickering were music to her ears.

Jordyn—used to tuning out the idiocy of her siblings—continued as if they hadn't interrupted. "As we speak, Blue is flying to New York."

"Why?" Spencer frowned. His first reaction was irrational. He had no business asking. However, he didn't like the idea of Blue leaving Seattle without his knowledge.

"Tomorrow, three Cyclone players are attending an MLB-sponsored charity event."

Spencer nodded. Any charity that benefited children was hard for him to pass up. He'd attended this one on several occasions. Though asked, this year he couldn't swing it this time. He had too much on his plate.

"Blue works for the Cyclones. MLB handles all the PR for this event. Why is she going?"

"Exactly Blue's question. Vance wants her to, and I quote, 'hold the player's hands and make certain they don't say anything that will reflect poorly on the team.'"

"That's a load of bogus crap," Spencer muttered.

"I agree," Jordyn nodded. "So does Blue. However, she wasn't left with a choice. Vance is her boss. He said go. So…"

"Blue went."

"There *is* a silver lining. The three Cyclones are major hotties." Jordyn directed her comment to the women at the table. "Especially Jalen Reardon. I advised Blue to make the most of a bad situation."

"Do you think Blue would…? You know." Evelyn waggled her eyebrows. Quiet by nature, Rick's wife nonetheless had a wicked sense of humor which could surface at any moment.

"A one-night stand? Blue?" With a wave of her hand, Dorothy dismissed the idea. "She's on a business trip and will conduct herself accordingly."

Silently, Spencer agreed with his mother. And cheered her for voicing her opinion. Until Dorothy went and spoiled it by adding a codicil to her original thought.

"However, I agree with Jordyn. Jalen Reardon is all kinds of yummy."

"Mom!"

Rick sounded shocked—and more than a little embarrassed—that his mother would say such a thing. Wisely, Spencer kept his thoughts to himself.

"Don't be such a stick in the mud, Richard."

"Dad. Are you hearing this?"

"Your mother's right. She wants to enjoy a little man candy. So what?" Byron winked at his wife. "She never grouses when I admire Jennifer Lopez's shapely backside. So, who am I to complain?"

"Blue should go for it," Millie piped in.

"You think so?" Reid asked his wife.

"Why not? Though I agree with Dorothy. Blue should wait until they're back in Seattle. Having sex on the team's dime would be tacky."

"What do you think, Spencer?"

Meeting his sister's wide-eyed gaze, Spencer thought he'd like to give Jordyn a swift kick in the pants. He knew damned well the game she played. Mention Blue's sex life and see what kind of rise she could get out of him.

Staring back, Spencer sent a silent message. *Nice try, brat. You took your best shot. But no cigar.*

"Consider me Switzerland."

"There's no such thing as neutrality in this family. Everybody has an opinion—and never fails to express it."

This time when Spencer looked at Jordyn, his eyes held a warning. *Keep pushing at your own peril, little sister.*

Wisely, Jordyn decided to err on the side of caution. She dropped the subject. At least for now.

Later that evening, his body happy from good food and even better company, Spencer crawled into bed ready—and expecting— a good night's sleep. However, his brain had other ideas. His thoughts flew right, then left. Up, then down. Never settling. A million little things kept his brain from relaxing as if trying to avoid the one thing that really kept him awake.

All that talk about Blue and New York. Inevitably, it had stirred up memories.

Giving up, Spencer sighed. Punching his pillow, he lay on his back, focusing on the ceiling before closing his eyes. Slowly, as if savoring the pictures in a forgotten photo album, he allowed his mind to drift to another place. Another time.

Blue's *first* visit to New York. Or rather, the events that led up to the trip.

CHAPTER SEVEN

SIX YEARS EARLIER

"ONE OF MY best friends is having a day after, the day after, New Year's Eve party in New York."

Blue, snuggled next to Spencer, raised her head just enough to give him a quick kiss on the chin.

"The fact that you said that with a straight face makes me wonder how much life in the big leagues has warped your sense of what's normal."

"I admit it's strange. But so is Crack."

"Crack? As in the sound the bat makes when it meets a baseball?"

"So smart." Spencer kissed Blue's temple. "Though the how and why of Crack's name isn't the point."

"Right. Party. To which you were invited." Sitting up, Blue untangled her arms from around Spencer's waist, removing her leg from where it draped over his. "We've been dating exactly…" Blue checked her watch. "Three weeks, two days, thirteen hours, and seven minutes."

"What about the spare seconds?"

"Let's not get anal. On the other hand." Blue paused. Her eyes twinkled. As if considering the prospect, she turned her head, right then left. "Nope. Though a young man once asked me to give it a go and tried to make it sound like a transcendental experience, I pass. The appeal eludes me."

"Who asked?"

"Out of bounds, bud. We agreed. What we've done. *Who* we've done. Off limits."

Blue made the suggestion on their second date, soon after they realized there would be a third. And fourth. And more. Spencer seconded the idea—wholeheartedly.

Spencer cupped Blue's face. His eyes went to her mouth as his thumb traced her bottom lip. Air, warm and sweet, escaped her mouth. How had they gotten here, he wondered?

One unexpected, mind-altering, life-changing kiss was all it took. One second Blue was a friend who annoyed him as often as she made him laugh. The next, he couldn't stop thinking about her.

When Spencer was alone, those thoughts were of a graphic nature that not so long ago, he'd have deemed highly inappropriate.

When Blue was with him, he had to touch her. He needed her kisses like a plant needs the sun. Her lips warmed him—inside and out.

Yet—for reasons he couldn't explain—Spencer hadn't made a move to take their relationship to the next level. Blue was a woman. Mature, willing, and fully capable of knowing what she wanted. No question about it. She made it clear that she wanted him.

Something had to give—and soon.

Part of Spencer's reluctance—the part he could identify—had to do with the lack of privacy due to their respective living arrangements.

Though initially surprised, nobody in his family had raised an objection when they found out Spencer and Blue's relationship had turned romantic. Something told him that would change if he asked if Blue could stay the night. With him. In his childhood bedroom.

Blue had the same problem. Her dorm was closed for the holidays. And though Connie and Clark O'Hara seemed fine with Spencer's new role in their daughter's life, he doubted they'd condone a sleepover.

Three weeks, two days, thirteen hours, and seven minutes— Blue wasn't the only one keeping track. They'd shared countless kisses. Night after night, they steamed up the windows of a borrowed Chevy sedan. By heart, Spencer knew the shape, feel, delectable taste of Blue's lovely, perfectly shaped breasts.

"You're a tease, Spencer Kraig," Blue told him last night as he walked her to the door.

Spencer could see the frustration in her eyes. Hear it in her voice. Since he felt the same, he sympathized.

"Our first time won't be in the back of a car."

Blue took Spencer's hand, lacing her fingers with his. She

kissed the back of his hand and shrugged. "I had a solution, but you shot me down."

"The bathroom at the *Dairy Queen*? How is that possibly better than the back of my brother's old Chevy?"

"Maybe not better. But it's private."

Spencer pulled Blue close, his hand rubbing her back. "A restaurant bathroom isn't private."

"Depends on the time of day. I worked there one summer. I can attest to the fact that during the afternoon lull, from around two-thirty until four, that bathroom saw a lot of action." Blue, always happy to cuddle as close as possible, rested her head on Spencer's chest. "Want me to name names?"

Chuckling, Spencer shook his head. "Maybe some other time."

"Fine. But that doesn't solve our problem." Lifting her head, Blue met his gaze, a frown furrowing her brow. She had a touch of vulnerability in her eyes that he'd never seen before. "Unless you don't want me that way?"

"You know better than that." Spencer kissed her softly. "We'll get there, Blue. Right time. Right place."

Tonight, Blue had insisted on making all the plans. She picked him up in her little compact car—long on gas mileage, short on space—driving to an area near the UW campus. She didn't stop at a restaurant as Spencer expected but instead parked outside an apartment complex.

"Did I miss something?" Spencer asked. "I thought we were going out to dinner."

"We are. Here. For some reason, I'd forgotten that my friend and her roommate had left town for the holidays. Our conversation last night reminded me."

Blue took Spencer's hand, leading the way into the building and up two flights of stairs. Places like this were found on campuses all over the country. Probably the world. Student housing. Inexpensive and nondescript.

On each side of a carpet-lined hall was a series of white doors. Blue stopped at number three-fourteen.

"Ta da!" She said, throwing the door open with a flourish. "Instant privacy."

Not entering, Spencer craned his neck, looking right, then left. The renters had added a few splashes of color to brighten up the utilitarian design.

"Come on," Blue laughed, tugging Spencer into the room. "There are some takeout menus on the counter. Order a pizza. Or Chinese. Whatever sounds good to you."

"Takeout?" Spencer asked, tongue firmly planted in his cheek. "Aren't you going to cook?"

"Sure. Let's see." Blue opened a cupboard. "We have stale saltines and…" She stuck her head in the fridge. "A moldy lump that at one time might have been cheese. Rachael Ray, eat your heart out."

Blue was a beautiful young woman. A dream walking. But Spencer could find that on the pages of any fashion magazine. Her wit, intelligence, and innate kindness had Spencer on the brink of falling—hard.

"I'll grab us something to drink. Jackie isn't big on buying food, but she and Shayla always keep the fridge stocked with other essentials. What would you like? Beer? Coke?"

"Beer. Thanks," Spencer answered absently.

Mind spinning, Spencer took out his phone. He called a local pizza parlor, placing their order while trying to sort through his thoughts. Talk about a revelation.

Spencer was on the brink of falling in love with Blue.

Love. Was it the reason he wanted to slow things down? The reason he always stopped when they were on the brink of having sex? Because Spencer knew—deep in his heart—that when it came to Blue, nothing was casual.

In the past, Spencer enjoyed a woman's body, able to walk away without a backward glance. Not this time. Not with Blue.

Which brought him back to the here and now. A half-eaten pizza sitting on the table. His hand caressing Blue's cheek. Her eyes a warm, mellow gray. She looked happy. Happy to be with him. And Spencer felt the same.

"You plan on going to your friend's party. In New York." Blue smiled. "I'll miss you."

"Not if you come along."

"Me? To New York? With you?"

Smiling at Blue's amazed expression, Spencer nodded.

"Yes, yes, and yes. You don't have to be back at school until next week. I leave for Florida around the same time. This is a perfect chance for us to get away before our schedules get crazy."

"That's right. Spring Training starts this month." Blue shifted her gaze, a sure sign she wasn't telling him the absolute truth. "We've been having so much fun, I hadn't thought beyond right now."

"The thought hadn't crossed your mind that from now until October, my time will be strictly regimented?"

"Again. I'll miss you."

Unlike the first time Blue said the words, her smile wasn't as convincing.

"You won't get rid of me that easily, Bluebell." As he smoothed back her hair, Spencer's expression softened. He wasn't ready to say the words, but he hoped when Blue looked into his eyes she could see a little of what he felt. "It will take some work to keep this thing going. If you're willing, so am I."

"Yes." Blue threw herself at him, her arms winding around his neck. She peppered his face with quick kisses. "Yes, yes, yes. To everything. Us. New York. Next week. Next month. Yes."

"I'll take that as a yes." Rolling onto his back, Spencer took Blue with him until the length of her blanketed him. "We can do this, Blue."

Blue nodded, her cheek rubbing his, her lips brushing his ear. Taking the lobe between her teeth, she bit ever so lightly, then whispered, "Yes."

"Want to watch a movie?"

The question was ridiculous under the circumstances. Spencer meant it that way because he knew it would make Blue laugh. The sound tickled his ear. And as always, it warmed his blood while simultaneously lightening his heart.

"Another time." Rising, Blue straddled his hips, her hands braced on his chest. "I have a better idea. To combat your apparent shyness—who would've guessed—we'll play a game."

Spencer could have argued. Him? Shy? Talk about ridiculous. Since he knew she was teasing—and the view from his vantage point was so nice—he kept his thoughts to himself.

Besides, he was all but certain the kind of game Blue had in mind would be right up his alley.

"Shyness can debilitate a person. To combat the problem, we'll take things slow and easy. That is where the game comes in. It's called *Touch Me Here*."

"Sounds intriguing." Shifting slightly, Spencer aligned Blue's jeans-covered center with his. Hot didn't begin to describe the feeling. When she gasped, he smiled slowly. "What are the rules?"

"Simple. Place your hand on my body."

"Where?"

"Your choice. But," Blue cautioned. "You can only leave it there for a little while. I don't want you to be overwhelmed."

"I appreciate your kind consideration."

Slowly, Spencer looked Blue up and down. Enjoying the game, he chose a spot, noting the surprise that flitted across her face.

"I've always been a leg man," he explained, squeezing Blue's thigh.

"Five seconds."

"And then?" His hand moved, to the inside of her leg.

"Pick another spot."

They went on this way for several minutes—or was it hours? Spencer wasn't sure. At some point, fun became a kind of torture. Especially when Blue would wiggle her hips. He didn't know if her intention was to grind against his growing erection, but the way her lips curved upward made him suspicious.

"Wouldn't it be more fun if you took off your shirt?" Spencer asked, his hand hovering over Blue's breast.

Looking skeptical, Blue frowned. "Are you sure you're ready for that?"

"Oh, I think I can handle it."

"Okay. But just—"

"For a little while," Spencer finished. "I know."

Blue dispensed with her shirt, followed quickly by her bra, the garment flying over her shoulder in a blur of purple lace.

Spencer wasn't about to remind her that all he asked for was the shirt. Nor did he hesitate to take advantage of the unexpected bonus. Cupping Blue's breast, his sigh answered hers. So soft. So firm. Saliva pooled in his mouth in anticipation of his first taste.

"I don't want to play anymore," Blue exclaimed

The rhythm of her breathing increased, her eyes closing in pleasure as Spencer rubbed his callused palm across the tender, hardened tips.

"Hold on."

Spencer didn't have to ask twice. As he stood, Blue's legs tightened their grip. She pressed her breasts against him, her fingers finding purchase in his thick hair.

"Bedroom?" he asked, kissing the side of her neck.

"Sounds good." Blue tilted her head, giving Spencer better access.

Chuckling, Spencer skirted the sofa. The room was small. Kitchen to the left. Leaving the darkened doorway to the right as the only logical direction for him to take.

At the end of the hall, Spencer found just enough light to guide his way. He shouldered his way through the open door. One bedroom. One king-sized bed. Interesting.

"Jackie and Shayla are lovers," Blue said as if reading his thoughts. She leaned over, turning on the end-table lamp. "Does that bother you?"

"No, Bluebell." Spencer pulled back the covers, setting her on the bed. Kneeling, he took off her socks, kissing one instep, then the other. "Gay, straight. I don't care. Sex should be between consenting adults. After that, I say live and let live."

Blue threw her arms around Spencer, tumbling him to the bed. Beaming, she touched his face.

"I'm so glad. I could never have sex with a known homophobe. It would've killed me to kick you out. But I'm a woman of principles. It's best you know that now before we take this any further."

Spencer continued undressing Blue.

"That's the difference between us," he said, sliding her jeans down her long legs.

"You don't have principles?"

"I do. And I'd kick you out of bed if I discovered you were a prejudiced asshole." He paused, his lips savoring the soft skin just below Blue's bellybutton. "*After* we had sex."

Blue's laugh turned to a gasp as Spencer moved lower, spreading her legs. Raising his gaze, he paused when saw the passion in her eyes mixed with something else.

Not fear. But what? Unease? Wariness? Spencer stopped. This

wouldn't do.

Fully dressed, he joined Blue on the bed, taking her into his arms, a soothing hand on her shoulder.

"You okay?"

"Great. All's good. Keep going."

Blue liked using her words. Spencer liked hearing them. Three stilted sentences would be fine—great—if his touch had scrambled her brain to a point beyond coherent speech. But he could tell a wobbly mind wasn't her problem.

Always direct, when Blue's eyes wouldn't meet his, Spencer knew something was wrong.

"Talk to me, Blue."

"I… It's nothing really. Why are you wearing so many clothes?"

Blue tugged at the hem of his t-shirt. With a hand over hers, Spencer stayed her almost frantic movements.

"Look at me."

With a sigh, Blue's gaze moved from Spencer's chest, stopping at his chin.

"My eyes, Bluebell. Look me in the eyes."

Slowly, Blue complied, grumbling something under her breath.

"What was that?" Spencer asked, lips twitching. He was well aware of what she said.

"Don't call me Bluebell," she hissed.

The color in her cheeks, the flare of anger turning her irises a stormy gray. Much better.

"Then tell me what's going on in that complicated mind of yours."

"Complicated? Really?" Blue's frown turned contemplative. Then her expression brightened. Apparently, after some thought, she decided to take it as a compliment.

"And sexy as hell," Spencer assured her. Smoothing back her hair, he ran his hand down the silky length, his fingers curling around the ends. "If you aren't ready for this, Blue, we'll wait. But you have to tell me what you're feeling. Always. No matter what. I'll do the same. As long as we can talk things out, we'll be fine."

Sighing, Blue nodded.

"Everything was great. It still is," she said.

"But…?"

"When you started to… "

"Go down on you?"

"Yes." A flush covered Blue's cheeks. "God. I hate this. I'm not a blushing virgin. But I may not be as experienced as I've led you to believe."

Blue hadn't led Spencer anywhere. He didn't know how many men she'd been with or what she'd done or hadn't done. Still, he could tell when they kissed, when they touched, that she retained a certain innocence no amount of attitude could mask.

"I want you, Blue." More than he'd once thought possible. Spencer took her hand, raising it to his lips. "Do you want me?"

"Yes." Blue's grip was almost as fierce as the look in her eyes. "It's different with you, Spencer. I don't know how to describe it. More intense. More exciting. More… terrifying."

"I was with you up until that last one." The last thing Spencer wanted was to frighten her.

"*You* don't terrify me," Blue collapsed onto the mattress. Spencer went with her, propping himself up on one elbow. "*I* terrify me. All of a sudden, I realized that I'm out of my league. Don't get me wrong. I like sex. It's fun. And feels good—most of the time."

"I should hope so." If some idiot hurt Blue—even if it were unintentional—he wanted names.

"Fun and vanilla. That's about the sum of my experience. I was fine with that. Until now. I'm afraid of not knowing how to please you. That after all the beautiful, sophisticated, blowjob giving, *Kama Sutra* expert women you've been with, I'll be a big, fat disappointment."

"Now *I'm* terrified. And a little insulted," Amazed, Spencer shook his head. "You were supposed to be thinking about how good I made you feel. Instead, all that crap was running through your head? Good thing my ego is capable of taking a slap or two."

"Spencer…"

Spencer stopped Blue with a look. "My sex life isn't a series of kinky free-for-alls. I don't have a trapeze hanging from my bedroom ceiling. As for the *Kama Sutra*? Have you ever looked at that thing?"

Blue shook her head.

"Ninety-five percent of those positions look more painful than pleasurable. The others are pretty routine."

"Oh."

Blue looked chastised. She also looked intrigued. Spencer laughed.

"One of these days we'll check it out. Together. For now, let's get one thing straight. I don't need or want you to be anything but yourself. Explain the blowjob comment. Have you? Haven't you?"

"Once." From the look on Blue's face, she didn't find the memory pleasant. "After a lot of jamming and ramming, I was out. I told him to buy an inflatable doll and leave us flesh-and-blood women alone."

Damn, Spencer thought, she was spectacular.

"Got it. Not a fan of blowjobs."

"I didn't say that," Blue quickly corrected. "I might like it— with the right man. With you."

Spencer's gaze fell to Blue's mouth. The image was easy to see. With regret, he sighed. Another time. For now, they'd concentrate on the basics.

"You like sex." Spencer gave Blue a gentle kiss. "I like sex." Another kiss, longer, more intense. "Any reason we shouldn't like sex with each other?"

"I'm game if you are."

"No more games. This is about to get serious."

Going to his knees, Spencer whipped off his shirt. A second later, the rest of his clothes were on the floor. Blue's eyes widened.

Spencer rarely considered how his body looked. Keeping in shape was part of his job. The more he fine-tuned his engine and all the running parts, the better they performed as a whole.

However, Spencer liked looking at Blue. She was a beautiful woman. It gave him a surge of pleasure knowing she felt the same about him. Though by the changing of her breathing and the darkening of her irises, the answer was obvious, he had to ask.

"Like what you see?"

Blue reached out, her hand hovered near his abs for an instant, and then she snatched it back.

"Now who is the shy one?" Spencer's tone teased, but the green of his eyes told a different story. He wanted Blue's touch. Desperately. "If you want something, reach out and take it."

Slowly, but confidently, Blue traced the well-defined ridges of Spencer's abdomen.

"I want you," Blue said in a breathy voice.

"Then I'm yours."

Spencer lowered his body over Blue. Warm flesh to warm flesh. In no hurry to do more than allow himself to savor the feeling, he nuzzled her neck, breathing in her scent, committing every moment to memory.

Blue's hands caressed his back. Slowly, as if she too wanted to remember. Spencer closed his eyes. This wasn't sex, he realized.

For the first time in his life, Spencer was about to *make love*. And he found the revelation heady. Exhilarating.

And yes, a little terrifying.

Loving Blue. Nice ring to it.

Spencer nudged her legs apart, testing if she was ready for him. Hot and slick. Perfect. With one long, slow glide, he joined their bodies. His hands framed Blue's face, his eyes held her gaze. She gasped the pleasure and wonder right there for him to see.

Spencer felt a growing need for release, but he wasn't ready for it to end. Blue's legs gripped his hips, perfectly matching his rhythm. Rising higher. Higher. The trip was a heady ride.

Over the top, they fell together in a burst of bright lights and exploding jolts of electricity.

Rolling to his side, taking Blue with him, Spencer imagined how they'd look if somebody took a picture. A wild mess of tangled sheets and tangled limbs. Sweaty bodies clinging together.

He glanced down at Blue.

Who needed a camera?

Spencer knew that the smile on Blue's face—content, radiant—would be burned into his brain for the rest of his life.

CHAPTER EIGHT

PRESENT DAY

A REASONABLE WOMAN would be on her way home to a hot shower, a large glass of wine, and a marathon session of *I Love Lucy*. All things that put Blue in her happy zone.

The trip to New York went smoothly. At least the part with the Cyclone players. The men were professional on camera. Charming. Engaging. In other words, there had been no reason for Blue to be there.

Blue wished she'd had time to take the players up on their offer to buy her lunch. After arriving at the hotel with just enough time to freshen up, change her clothes, and rush to the television studio—where she basically stood around and twiddled her thumbs—a leisurely hour or two with three charming, handsome men would have been nice.

Unfortunately, Blue's itinerary didn't leave time for a snack in the green room. An entire meal where she could sit down and get to know a few of the players she'd be working with during the next baseball season was out of the question.

The second the Cyclones' segment of *The Today Show* ended, Blue rushed to the hotel, grabbed her bag, checked out, barely making her flight back to Seattle.

Blue only had herself to blame. Vance Sutter wanted her to cry uncle. She was determined to stoically take whatever the jackass had to hand out. When she saw the ridiculously tight schedule he had her on, she should have protested. Instead, she took it as a challenge. She'd make every flight, do her job, and be in the office, at her desk, bright and early tomorrow morning.

Two years of this? Even if Blue lucked out and made every flight—given the vagaries of modern travel, such unprecedented punctuality wasn't likely—there would come the point when her body and mind gave out. No matter how tough she was physically and mentally, she was only human.

Blue won—she could call her trip a victory. She'd beaten Vance and his evil plan. This time. However, as she sat in the back of the taxi, a wrinkled, wilted mess, she questioned her strategy.

Should she stick out her current situation? Or would it be smarter to go over Vance's head and voice her concerns now before things got further out of hand?

Blue needed another perspective. One she trusted. So, instead of heading to her downtown condominium, she gave the taxi driver Jordyn's Queen Anne Hill address.

"Today sure was mild for mid-January," the driver chirped.

Unlike Blue, it seemed Josiah Ronald had gotten a good night's sleep. She blinked her bloodshot eyes. The driver picked her up at the airport well after the sun was down. For the life of her, she couldn't figure out why he felt it necessary to rub her nose in the fact that she hadn't been here for the nice January day.

"Sorry I missed it," Blue mumbled.

"Got to take these moments when they come. Stop and smell the roses. Life's too short."

The driver's statement—no matter how annoying and cliché riddled—was prophetic. Blue was only a few months into her dream job. She wouldn't say it had turned into a nightmare. But the excitement had dimmed.

Life *was* too short. Spending a good portion of it frustrated— bordering on miserable—didn't make any sense. Blue was young. Educated. She had a stellar resume. Finding another job wouldn't be a problem.

Except another job wouldn't be *the* job. Blue understood that quitting so soon wasn't an option. She needed a way to turn going to the office back into an enjoyable experience.

The taxi pulled to a stop outside a charming late nineteenth-century brownstone. Newly renovated, it retained the charm of a time gone by, yet sparkled with a modern coat of love and care.

The building emphasized the difference in Blue's and Jordyn's tastes. Best friends through and through, they nonetheless had opposite ideas of what made a home.

Blue craved modern comforts. The view of the city out of her large, floor-to-ceiling windows. Granite countertops. Stainless steel appliances.

She loved having a concierge in the lobby of her building. The underground parking garage. The fact that one phone call and somebody picked up her dry cleaning, seemingly returning it magically to her closet—no fuss, no muss.

Modern living at its best.

Technically, the condominium didn't belong to Blue. When a friend of her mother decided to move to California to be closer to her son and new granddaughter, she'd generously agreed to let Blue move in. She paid rent, the monthly condo fees, electricity, water, etc.

If at some future date Blue decided she wanted to make the condo her permanent home, the rent paid to that point would be deducted from the purchase price.

With all her expenses, Blue still shelled out less than she would for an apartment in the same area. A bonus was the fact that because of the downtown location, Cyclone Stadium was only a few blocks away. During the season, she could walk to all home games.

A sweet deal under any circumstances.

Jordyn was more about old-world charm than convenience. Not that she lived in the Stone Age. Indoor plumbing was a must. And she couldn't survive without a dishwasher and ice from the little nook in her refrigerator.

However, Jordyn preferred the feel of the historic Queen Ann Hill to the hustle and bustle of a more modern downtown location. She wanted to know her neighbors. Take a walk in the nearby park. Shop for her food at the little corner store located across the street.

The differences in Blue and Jordyn's tastes were proof that two people didn't have to agree on everything to get along. They were truly kindred spirits when it came to things that mattered. Loyalty. A sense of fair play. Honesty, whenever possible. Core values instilled in them by their parents.

Friendship, like any relationship worth having, took work. Blue and Jordyn argued. They hit the occasional bump. But one fact remained constant—irrefutable since the day they met.

Blue and Jordyn were sisters in every way but blood.

As she picked up her bag, Blue looked at the steps that led to the front door and sighed. She must be tired. Normally, she zipped up the brick and mortar without a second thought. Today, they looked like a mountain.

"Need a hand?"

Startled, Blue dropped her suitcase, letting out a yelp that to her ears had all the force of an undernourished kitten. She knew that voice. With a sigh, she turned her head.

Spencer. Naturally, when she was at her worst, he looked like an advertisement for a health spa. She could have posed for the before pictures. Spencer, the after.

"What are you doing here?"

"I could ask the same of you." Spencer picked up the sturdy carryon—the one Blue had owned since college—giving it the once over. Recognition sparked in his eyes, but he didn't comment. "Why are you back so soon? And why do you look like you were pulled behind the plane by a long rope? I know the economy sucks, but come on. The Cyclones can afford a seat inside."

"You'll have to forgive me if I don't laugh. I left my sense of humor at the Phoenix airport."

"You flew out of New York to Phoenix?"

"Via Chicago." Blue started up the steps. If Spencer wanted to follow, let him. She was too tired to worry about it.

"What the hell, Blue." Spencer easily reached the top ahead of her. Punching in the security code, he waited, holding open the door. "When did you leave New York?"

"Around noon."

Spencer did the math. "It took you nine hours? How did you come? By covered wagon?"

"You should write these down, Spencer. If the baseball thing doesn't work out, you can take your comedy routine on the road."

Closing the door behind them, Spencer set down the suitcase.

When Blue swayed a little to the right, he took her arm, leading her to the living room sofa.

"You look like hell. Sit down before you fall on your face."

"There's that charm I remember so well." Blue was exhausted, but she could still spew some sarcasm when the situation dictated it.

Gently, Spencer pushed her onto the sofa.

"I'll make you a cup of tea."

"I'd rather have a shot of that excellent Irish whiskey Jordyn keeps for special occasions."

"Any kind of alcohol, excellent or not, will knock you out like a light. Tea. The herbal crap Jordyn is always pushing."

Blue dropped her head onto the back cushion. Now that she was settled in a familiar, comfortable spot, her depleted reserves faded fast.

"I'll take a cup of green tea. I've had enough crap on every level the last few days to last me for some time." She yawned. "Where's Jordyn? And why are you here?"

"Unexpected business trip. There's some woman in the wilds of Whidbey Island who has a cream Jordyn has to get the rights to. As for me? I'm here strictly as forced labor. Seems there's a mirror that needs hanging."

"Right. And it's lotion, not cream," Blue corrected.

"What the hell is the difference?"

"Quite a bit, according to Jordyn. I think she mentioned the woman lives on Bainbridge Island."

"For the sake of her business, I hope my sister reels in her latest concoction. Otherwise, lotion, cream, or whichever damned island, I don't really give a flying leap." Spencer handed Blue a steaming mug, careful that she had a firm grip on the handle before letting go. "You can call her if it's important."

"I needed to vent. That's always best done in person."

As Spencer joined her, Blue's eyes narrowed when she noted the glass in his hand contained a splash of that very fine whiskey.

"Vent away," he said from his side of the sofa.

"Thanks just the same, I'll wait for Jordyn."

"You used to tell me your troubles."

Blue froze, the cup halfway to her lips. She used to tell Spencer everything. She thought he did the same. Turned out she was mistaken. The lesson had been hard learned. One she wasn't about to forget.

Taking a sip of tea, Blue shook her head.

"I should go."

Spencer looked as if he wanted to say something. Whatever changed his mind, Blue was grateful. She wasn't up to a sparring match.

"Let me drive you home."

"Would it do me any good to argue?"

"Waste of energy. Something you're low on at the moment."

The *as the crow flies* trip wasn't a long one. But the traffic that time of night added a good thirty minutes. Spencer was a skilled driver. Buckled into his low-riding Porsche, Blue closed her eyes and relaxed. Trust was still an issue between them, but not when it came to him behind the wheel.

"I'll be leaving for Arizona in few days."

"Mm. Spring Training. I'm well aware."

There were several team-sponsored events in which the players took part—on the few and far between off days. Come March, Blue would collect her frequent flyer miles to and from Arizona, making certain the PR side of the activities ran smoothly.

"Could we have dinner one night before I leave?"

Blue's eyes popped open.

"Why?"

"There are still a few things we need to talk about. Things I need to say." Spencer stopped outside Blue's building.

"I don't agree." Blue unbuckled her seatbelt. "Not that long ago, I couldn't imagine sitting in a car with you. We've made a lot of progress in a short amount of time."

"You deserve an apology."

"Do I?" Blue asked, curious to hear what Spencer had to say.

"The way I ended things. I…" he sighed. "I broke your heart."

What could Blue say? When he was right, he was right.

"Leaving you wasn't a decision I took lightly."

Blue waited, expecting—needing more. It didn't come.

"I was hurt. There were a few days when I didn't want to get out of bed." *More like a month.* "My heart broke. But not for the reason you think."

Before Spencer could respond, Blue jumped from the car. Adrenaline carried her into the lobby, across the marble floors, and into the elevator. She punched the button harder than necessary.

Damn, him, Blue cursed. With relish. Since she had the elevator to herself, she let loose a stream of words that would have impressed the most dedicated potty mouth.

Then Blue remembered her suitcase was still in Spencer's trunk. With a frustrated growl, she began a fresh tirade.

Blue was running on fumes. Sleep was out of the question until she calmed down. So, with a glass of her favorite Chablis sitting on the counter, she shed her jacket, the thought of a shower already loosening the bunched muscles in her shoulders.

Unfastening the button at her waist, Blue started to shimmy the pants over her hips just as the intercom to the lobby buzzed. She considered ignoring it but quickly dropped the idea—no matter how tempting.

With a sigh, Blue walked across the room, hitching up her pants as she went.

"Yes?" Blue asked.

"There's a Mr. Spencer Kraig here to see you, Ms. O'Hara."

Oh, for the love of God. Blue leaned against the wall, her eyes closing. The venting of her spleen had taken a lot out of her. The last thing she wanted was to go another round with Spencer.

"Tell him to go away, Rhonda."

"Give me the phone." Spencer's voice carried to Blue.

"He wants to speak with you."

Acting as an intermediary was part of the concierge's job description. However, Blue understood very well how stubborn Spencer could be when he wanted something. Rhonda was no match for his charm and determination.

"Put him on."

"Blue—"

"Go home, Spencer. Whatever you have to say can wait until morning. Make an appointment with my assistant. Or better yet, do me a favor. Keep it to yourself."

"I don't want to meet at your office."

"Too bad," Blue interjected. Great. Now on top of everything else, her head had started to pound.

"You should've stayed in the car so we could finish our conversation."

Blue sighed. She recognized Spencer's *I'm not budging until I get my way* tone. Too bad. He could rot in the lobby for the rest of the night for all she cared.

"Imagine the headline," Spencer continued as if he could read her mind. "*Cyclones player arrested for disturbing the peace.* How well do you think it will sit with management when they find out I picked up in the lobby of *your* building?"

Blue felt her stomach clench. Spencer hit her most vulnerable spot. Well, she wasn't giving in that easily. He might know how to get to her. But he seemed to forget. Unless something big had changed in four years, she knew his most vulnerable spots as well.

"Fine. Get yourself arrested. What will your mother say?"

Spencer paused, making Blue smile.

"Low blow, Bluebell."

"Right back at you, Jackass."

"I'm sorry I threatened you. We both know I never would've followed through. Please let me come up."

Suddenly, Blue wanted to cry. The culmination of a crappy, tension-filled business trip, little sleep, little to eat, and now, the soothing sound of Spencer's voice. He wasn't trying to manipulate or charm.

Utterly Sincere Spencer. He couldn't fake it. He never tried. And it got her every time. Letting out a slow, pent-up breath, Blue's head fell back. She couldn't believe she was about to cave.

"Under one condition."

"Name it."

"Grab a couple of sub sandwiches from the place down the block."

"Gerry's? Italian special, right?"

"Right."

"I'll see you in few, Blue."

As she headed to the bathroom, determined to take her shower before Spencer arrived, Blue knew she shouldn't have been surprised. Gerry's had the best subs in the city. Naturally, Spencer would know the place. And of course, he knew which was her favorite.

Rather than taking her time as she originally planned, Blue downed a couple of aspirin before jumping under the hot spray of water. Raising her face, she braced her hands against the granite wall. If possible, her entire body let out a heartfelt hallelujah.

Five minutes later, Blue felt almost human again. She gave her body a quick covering of lotion. Fashioned her damp hair into a quick top knot. Slipping on a loose pair of linen drawstring pants and long-sleeved Seattle Knights' t-shirt, she'd just added some thick, bright yellow socks when the doorbell rang.

Blue looked at the clock, surprised at Spencer's speed.

This time of day, Gerry's was usually packed, the line sometimes stretching out the door even when cold and rainy. Though the service was speedy, fifteen minutes on a mild night was impressive.

Then again, this was Spencer Kraig, not the average guy off the street. Must be nice to be one of the best known and most popular athletes in the country. All he had to do was snap his fingers—or flash that famous smile—and lines of people literally parted in awe of his greatness.

In the face of that kind of constant adoration, a vast majority of the population would be impossible to be around. Spencer had a nice, fat healthy ego. But it had never bloated to the point where it turned insufferable.

At the slightest hint of such a thing, Spencer's family happily knocked him back down a peg or two.

"You smell good." Spencer's idea of greeting, he breathed deeply as he entered through the door. "Better than these sandwiches. And that's saying something."

Despite herself, Blue's lips twitched. Classic Spencer. He could throw out a compliment with utter ease, never sounding forced or too provocative. He had the gift. One he honed to perfection.

"The plates are in the cupboard next to the refrigerator. The glasses are—"

"I've got this, Blue. Sit. Relax. Do you want to eat at the dining table or in the living room?"

"Living room."

The simple acts of taking a shower and donning freshly laundered clothing had given Blue her second wind. Or was it her third? Maybe fourth? Either way, she no longer felt as if a strategically placed feather would knock her flat on her back.

A marathon was out of the question. However, if Spencer played nice, she could handle him.

As she made herself comfortable on the sandy gray sofa, Blue listened to Spencer's hummed rendition of *Uptown Funk*. He moved to the beat in his head, plating their sandwiches, setting them on a serving tray he rooted out from one of the cupboards. He added, napkins, her glass of wine was still sitting on the counter, and another he poured for himself.

Blue waited until Spencer joined her, taking the seat next to her.

"I don't have the energy—or patience—for a fight, Spencer."

Frowning, Spencer handed Blue her wine. He met her gaze, the green of his eyes a bright emerald. For an instant, she thought he would reach for her. Wisely—remembering he needed that hand to field baseballs—he reconsidered the impulse.

"We don't fight, Blue. At least we never did. We discuss—heatedly. We argue. We talk things through. But fight? Never."

When Blue didn't respond, Spencer's frown deepened.

"I'm right. Aren't I?"

Once—it seemed like forever ago—Blue would have agreed with Spencer. They talked about everything. On the phone. In person. Before sex. During. After.

Even when silent, they communicated by a touch. Or a look.

The easy rapport was gone. Smashed by Spencer's carelessness.

What to say? How to say it? After all this time, was any of it relevant? If Blue told Spencer what she thought he wanted to hear, would it stir up hurt and bitterness better left buried? Or would her honesty let them take the first steps toward truly moving on?

Blue wished she had the power to jump ahead in time. Just enough to see how everything worked out. If she found a mess, she could magically come back to this moment. Give herself a do-over.

But life didn't work that way. Blue had chosen her course of action and hope she made the right choice.

"Eat. You've had a hard day. We can talk later."

Maybe because Spencer decided to make the choice for her. Or maybe Blue was simply tired of thinking about the past. Dangling just out of sight. Never completely going away, no matter how she tried to convince herself otherwise.

Blue tossed aside her sandwich.

"I wanted a quiet night. By myself. Instead, you practically blackmailed me into letting you up here."

"That's a little harsh."

"Shut up." Blue stood, feeling the need to move. "You'll listen. Period. No comments. No unsolicited opinions." Stopping, she speared Spencer with her sharpened gaze. "I never had the chance to tell you off."

"I didn't handle it well."

"Really?" Blue asked, sure she must have misheard. "Not well? Talk about the understatement of the year. You broke up with me in person. Should I pat you on the back for that little—and I do mean little—gesture of decency? After two years, you show up on my doorstep with no warning and tell me it's over. You barely made it in the door before you were off to… Where was it? Texas? Colorado?"

"Chicago."

Gesturing with one hand, she used the other to grab her wine, taking a thoughtful sip.

"That's right. Chicago. You were in Colorado, detoured to Seattle, then jumped a plane to re-join your team."

"Not my finest hour."

Spencer had the good grace—the intelligence—to recognize the can of worms he'd opened. And the fact they couldn't go back. Blue had let him off easy during their meeting at her office.

This time, the gloves were off.

"I suppose I could've gone all crazy ex-girlfriend. I show up at your game. And what? Tears? Yelling? Naturally, I get escorted from the stadium. Some industrious photographer sells the pictures for a nice profit. The tabloids eat that kind of thing up." With a huff—easily picturing the mess—Blue raised her glass, gulping down half the contents. "Wouldn't that have provided a big laugh for you and your buddies?"

"You know better than that, Blue," Spencer sighed.

On a roll, Blue ignored him.

"I had my pride. You wounded it. Battered it—more than a bit. But like me, my pride bounced back—eventually."

"I said I was sorry."

You apologized for the wrong reason. Blue wanted to scream the words. But that wouldn't help. Taking a deep breath—her fingers dangerously close to snapping the stem of the wineglass— she searched for the right way to explain.

"Breaking up with me was your right, Spencer. The way you did it—crappy."

"Yes."

Confronted with his misdeeds, Spencer wasn't running. He sat and took what Blue handed out. No arguments. No excuses. She had to give him props for that.

"I was scared."

Blue had come to that conclusion long ago. Spencer's admission, quietly stated, his gaze steady—unwavering—surprised her. And pissed her off.

"Why didn't you say so at the time?"

Spencer shrugged. "I was scared."

"Don't you think I felt the same? I was twenty-two years old, Spencer. College was ending. I had decisions to make. Big fat, life-changing decisions." Scrubbing a hand over her face, Blue finished off her wine.

"Maybe you should take it easy, Blue."

Spencer tried to stop Blue when she replaced her empty glass with his, but for once, she was faster. Her vision blurred slightly, but with a few blinks, he came back into focus, as did her thoughts.

"We talked about everything? Isn't that what you said? Then, instead of blowing our relationship to bits, why didn't you come to me?" Blue blinked, this time to stay the tears she felt could fall at any second. "Why?"

Blue felt a burst of anguish—unsettlingly fresh after so many years. With a shuddering sigh, she collapsed onto the sofa.

"Because I was an idiot."

"That's a fact, Spencer. Not a reason."

Blue said the words as a statement. Not a joke. Spencer—to his credit—nodded solemnly.

"It's all I have to give you. I panicked. Plain and simple. I wasn't ready for whatever came next."

"So, you unilaterally broke things off. Without talking to me first."

Blue, on the downward side of her anger, looked Spencer directly in the eyes, willing him to understand.

Spencer swallowed hard. "In the car? Earlier? That is what you meant?"

Finally, Blue thought. Her mind and body simultaneously relaxed as if finally finding a modicum of peace. Closing her tired eyes, she leaned her head against the back of the sofa.

"You left without a word of explanation. Without *talking* to me. I didn't just lose my lover. I lost my friend. And *that* broke my heart."

"I wish…" Spencer paused. "When I should've spoken out, I didn't. I've apologized. Though I was sincere, does it matter? Is it too late? Will there ever be enough words to fix what I broke?"

Blue felt the cushion next to her shift. Eyes shut, she could imagine Spencer leaning closer, his expression intense. His eyes searching her face. Turning, she curled into a ball.

"I don't know. Maybe." Blue whispered. "I hope so."

"So do I. More than you can know."

Drifting off, Blue listened to the sound of Spencer rising, certain he was leaving. The feel of his arms, under her legs, around her waist, made her eyes fly open.

"What are you doing?"

"Putting you to bed. And before you argue—or make a foolish attempt to get away. Don't."

"Damn it, Spencer. I—"

"I said I'm putting you to bed. Period. What you do after that is your business."

In a few long strides, Spencer was in her bedroom, pulling aside the lace duvet. He settled her under the covers.

The bed felt wonderful. Much better than the sofa, Blue had to admit. Content, she settled in, her cheek resting on the soft, clean-smelling pillow case.

"I won't thank you." Though as every muscle in Blue's body relaxed, she was fairly certain her body would be eternally grateful.

"God forbid," Spencer said, his cough sounding suspiciously like a poorly camouflaged laugh. "Good night, Blue. Rest well. I'll see you in Arizona."

As she heard the bedroom door close with a light click, Blue frowned. She had two weeks to sort out her thoughts before she headed down to join the Cyclones.

The warm Arizona weather. Spring training. And Spencer.

In other words? Arizona? Good. Baseball? Better. And Spencer? Blue snuggled deeper under the covers.

Definitely, hope, she decided. Always a good thing.

CHAPTER NINE

"ARE THINGS GETTING any better at work?"

"More of a stalemate. Vance doesn't like me. But he hasn't made any overt moves since sending me to New York."

Jordyn shook her head. "You're okay with that?"

Blue had given her work situation a lot of thought. She wasn't giving up just because the job wasn't ideal. Not after all the time, planning, and effort she'd put into getting where she was.

"As long as Vance allows me a little breathing space to find my grove, he and I'll be fine."

"I hope so." Ever the protective friend, Jordyn didn't look convinced "However, if you want some advice on how to handle a difficult boss, this is the place to get it."

This place was the annual *Washington Women in Business* luncheon.

Each year women from all over the Pacific Northwest—not just the state of Washington—gathered to network, lend support, and enjoy an excellent meal.

Often, the point was to simply bask in the company of like-minded people with similar experiences and goals.

Jordyn never missed the event. This year, she talked Blue into coming along.

While in New York, Blue had attended something similar. She

hadn't been impressed by the large, unwieldy event. Everyone seemed to be in a hurry. Rubbernecking—not conversation—was the main event.

The goal? To trade up.

More than once, Blue had barely exchanged a perfunctory greeting before she was dropped for somebody more famous. Or influential. Or—in one case—a woman with better shoes.

"I'm still amazed that actually happened," Jordyn chuckled.

"It happened. Poor little me wore what I thought were a smashing pair of pale-yellow slingbacks. I was thrown over for Jimmy Choo. Black-patent leather. Four-inch stilettos," Blue said with a smile, sipping her sparkling water.

No alcohol today. Blue felt her stomach roil at the thought. After the other night, she was off the stuff for now. And the foreseeable future. The problem? Certainly not two measly glasses of wine—even with the empty stomach. The chaser of confessions was what had done her in

And the fact that Blue remembered every moment with a bright, stark, clarity. Though she felt a sense of relief—a lightening of a burden she'd carried around for four years—it mingled uneasily with an accompanying sense of trepidation.

What now? Blue had asked herself that question more than once in the past few days. Because one thing was certain. She'd been lying to herself for a long time. Time and heartache hadn't changed anything.

Blue still cared about Spencer. Deeply.

Unless, the contrary little devil on her shoulder argued, *Blue had simply fallen into a big vat of nostalgia.*

Whatever the answer, the feel of Spencer's arms around her as he carried her to bed had felt wonderfully familiar—and excitingly new. The look on his face. Gentle. Caring.

Blue hadn't imagined the want—the need—in Spencer's deep emerald eyes. Nor the answering response of her body. However, their love life had never been the problem. Just the opposite. The sex had been amazing. If she allowed her hormones to rule her head, she and Spencer could enjoy each other—no strings attached.

Casual relationships could be fun. And at this point in her life, Blue wasn't looking for anything more. Unfortunately, when it came to Spencer, it had always been all or nothing.

"We should find our seats," Jordyn said, unaware of the path of Blue's thoughts. "I think you'll be pleased with the women at our table."

"How do you know?" Since they'd purchased individual tickets—not an entire table—Blue assumed who their dining companions turned out to be was a crap shoot.

"It pays to have a friend on the seating committee."

"I smell a business deal in the making," Blue accused, a warm, knowing twinkle in her eyes.

With a wink, Jordyn smoothed a hand over her hair, the dark tresses falling past her shoulders in a sleek, straight line. Dressed to impress, her ivory-colored blouse, matching skirt, and red leather belt made her look professional yet at the same time, ultra-feminine.

"You know me well," Jordyn admitted as they weaved their way through the crowd. "Remember that cream I sent you for your birthday?"

"How could I forget? It makes my skin feel like satin."

"With no perfumes, dyes, or other impurities. We'll be sitting with the woman who created that magic concoction."

Well before she became a fan of the body cream, Blue had heard of the woman behind it. In a few short years, Claire Thornton had built a mini-empire. Her products were sold at high-end boutiques all over the world.

"Claire is launching a less expensive line. It will be in drug stores and supermarkets by the end of the year." Jordyn stopped when she found their table. "However, I'm after something exclusive. My stores only." Jordyn rubbed her hands together, a look of steely determination in her eyes. "Today is the beginning of my campaign."

"Looks like we're the first to arrive," Blue noted, pulling out her chair. The elegantly appointed table sat five, all the places currently empty.

"Here they come now," Jordyn indicated, nodding her head to a spot over Blue's shoulder.

Glancing to her right, Blue noticed the three women walking their way. A blonde and two brunettes. As her gaze focused on their faces—on one particular face—her eyes widened.

"Is that...?"

Jordyn nodded, knowing exactly who Blue meant.

"Riley Preston. Surprise!"

Blue clamped her teeth together to prevent her chin from hitting the table. Riley Preston. Genuine Seattle royalty. Owner of the Seattle Knights football team. And without a qualification, the woman Blue wanted to be when she grew up.

Though only a few years separated them, Riley Preston's accomplishments put women twice her age to shame. And the idea of anybody ever having the means to purchase a professional sports franchise was ridiculous to the extreme.

However, the way Riley conducted herself. Her business prowess and professional integrity. Those were the qualities Blue admired and aspired to. She had a million questions. With the huge lump in her throat, asking even one would be a challenge.

"Hello, ladies." Riley Preston smiled at Blue and Jordyn. "I'm sorry we're a little late. Just as we were walking out the door, Claire had a mommy emergency."

The blonde shrugged. "Babies don't care about fancy

luncheons. Gwen already enjoyed her meal. Unfortunately, Logan had just handed her to me when she felt the need to spit some of it up. It isn't the first time I had to change out of an expensive silk blouse."

"And it won't be the last time," the third woman added, her classically beautiful features lit with humor. "Next time it might be mud. Or apple sauce."

"Or motor oil from helping Daddy work on his car," Riley added, with a shake of her dark head, her lips quirked at the memory.

"Exactly. But mark my words, it will happen."

"You aren't late," Blue rushed to assure the women. The way they made their entrance—so funny and down to Earth—she felt a tad less intimidated. "We just arrived a little while ago."

"Good. As a woman who constantly emphasizes the importance of punctuality, it never looks good when I'm one of the last through the doors. I swear when Sean and I have an engagement, he'll dillydally just to drive me crazy."

Sean McBride, Blue thought. Legendary former Seattle Knights wide receiver. In all the excitement, she'd forgotten he was Riley Preston's husband. Lucky woman.

"Where are our manners?" Riley said. "We haven't introduced ourselves. My name is Riley Preston. The lady in the blue dress is Claire Thornton. And our friend in red is Dr. Violet Reed. Or do you prefer Benson? Violet is the only one of us to take her husband's name. Gaige insisted."

"Wrong. *I* insisted. Gaige was happy either way."

"It's a pleasure to meet you." Jordyn nodded to each woman. "I'm Jordyn Kraig. And this is my friend, Blue O'Hara."

"Wait. Blue?" Violet snapped her fingers. "Gaige—my husband—mentioned you the other day. Don't you work for the Cyclones?"

Gaige Benson mentioned her? Football God? In her opinion, the best quarterback in the history of the game? Feeling a little lightheaded, Blue grasped the edge of the table.

"Blue is part of the PR department," Jordyn answered for her tongue-tied friend. "She's in line for the top job—unless the jerk in charge has his way."

"It isn't that bad," Blue said quickly, sending Jordyn a warning look.

"Trouble with your boss?" Riley asked.

Blue hesitated. "We're still figuring each other out."

Riley laughed. "Very diplomatic. And smart. You shouldn't throw your boss under the bus. However, if you ever need any advice—or simply need to vent—feel free to call. I know what it's like to be a woman in a business dominated by arrogant, testosterone-laden, know-it-alls."

Taking Riley's card, Blue treated it like gold, carefully slipping it into her purse.

"You're accomplished, successful, smart, women. On top of that, you're married to sports rock stars."

"As Sean likes to remind me on a regular basis," Riley chuckled, the affection in her tone impossible to miss. "The man may be retired, but his ego is still going strong."

Blue couldn't help thinking about Spencer. He wasn't hers. But… Back when they were together, she occasionally wondered what life would be like married to a famous athlete. These women knew the answer. It seemed only natural to ask.

"How do you do it? Work. Family. Famous husbands? And Logan Price is still playing." Blue looked at Claire. "It can't be easy."

"I don't think there's one answer to that question," Claire said. "It helps that I love the game. And Logan. But don't let anybody fool you. Marriage is work."

"Amen," Violet added. "Mind you, when the man is the right one—and he feels the same about you—it's the best job ever."

"Our husbands. Our children. Our jobs. For each of us, it's different. But we have one major thing in common," Riley said, meeting the gaze of her friends. "We love. And we're loved in return. It doesn't get any better than that."

CHAPTER TEN

"MAN. WOULD YOU look at this? I have a fucking blister on my fucking blister. How the hell does that happen, Yoda?"

Spencer cringed. He had enough of his own aches and pains. The last thing he needed was to have somebody else's bloody foot shoved in his face. Especially one owned by a man whose sweaty cleats made the smell of rotten meat seem appetizing.

"Damn it, Kaminsky," Spencer shoved the two hundred and fifty-pound first baseman out of his way. "Take care of that before it gets infected."

Travis watched Kaminsky hobble toward the trainer's room. Shaking his head, he tossed his glove into the locker next to Spencer's.

"That dumbass and his rancid feet. Every spring it's the same routine."

"Every single spring for three years." Nick, his locker flanking Spencer's to the left, laid on the bench, his legs hanging over the end. "Makes you wonder why we do it."

"The women?" Travis offered.

"The money?" Spencer chimed in.

"The fame?" Nick offered.

Looking at his friends, Spencer caught their grins, adding one of his own. Women, money, and fame were nice. Hell, they were freaking fantastic. But they knew the real reason they put their bodies through the daily grind. Pure and simple. They did it for the love of the game.

Spencer learned baseball in the traditional manner. Father to son. Byron Kraig had a passion for the game. He nurtured his youngest son's talent every step of the way. Little League. High school. Two years of college. A brief stint in the minors.

On the day Spencer started his first professional game, Byron had been right there in the stands. Proud as a peacock.

Travis and Nick told different tales of their journey to *the show*. Each much less storybook than Spencer's. On the surface, they had little in common beyond baseball.

Yet for all their differences, Travis and Nick were his closest friends. And two of the best men he'd ever known. They knew most of his secrets. He knew a good percentage of theirs. Which was a good thing—most of the time.

At the moment, Spencer wished he'd kept certain things to himself. Especially anything and everything about Blue.

"Did you see the gorgeous redhead in the stands?" Travis asked, tossing his game-day jersey into the big hamper located about ten feet away. He hit his target. Most of his fellow teammates didn't bother, leaving their dirty uniforms littering the locker room floor.

"How could I miss her?" Nick rolled to his feet. "When the sun hit her, that hair glowed like a glorious beacon. Did you see her, Spence?"

How could he miss her? Blue—red hair or no red hair—stood out in any crowd. But rather than pander to Travis and Nick, he shrugged.

"Unlike you, I had my mind—and my eyes—on the field."

"True. Yoda's head is always in the game," Travis nodded. Glancing at Nick, his dark eyes danced with humor. "Between innings is another matter. Every time we left the field, Spence glanced toward the stands. Wonder why?"

Nick rubbed his chin, his expression exaggeratedly thoughtful. "Hm. That's a puzzler. Let me think."

Spencer rolled his eyes. And these were the men he called friends?

"Can it, assholes, or I'll get Kaminsky to stick his gunk-crusted foot in your faces."

Travis held up his hands in surrender. "I'm out."

"Wuss," Nick countered

No more jaunty taunts were sent Spencer's way. Understandable. As threats went, Kaminsky's foot was pretty horrific.

"Seriously, Spence. You need to make your move before somebody else beats you to it."

Somebody else? As in one of the Cyclones? Spencer didn't like the sound of that.

What the hell had Travis heard? As much as Spencer wanted to ask—Travis wanted it more. He wasn't getting pulled in.

"Blue can date who she chooses."

Not buying it, Travis surveyed the room. "You mean if she were to go out with say... I don't know. Drake Langford? You wouldn't care?"

"Langford's a good guy."

Spencer glanced at the rookie. The kid was a star in the making. But he was just that. A kid. Pretty. Well-built. Given a few years to mature, he might rise to Blue's level. At the moment, she was way out of Langford's league.

"How about Nick?"

"What?" Spencer's head whipped around, spearing Nick with his gaze.

"Me?" Nick's expression went from surprised to speculative.

"Since you weren't impressed by Langford, I upped the ante to somebody with a little more..." Travis paused as if searching for the right word.

"Sexual cachet?" Nick offered.

Travis nodded, obviously pleased by the suggestion.

"Give it a rest!" Spencer's raised voice drew more attention than he anticipated. He softened his tone, the perpetual locker room music camouflaging his words. "I get the point, Travis. But in case you weren't aware, Blue isn't down here to fill her social calendar. She has a job to do."

"What about after hours? There aren't any rules that prohibit her from dating a Cyclone." When Spencer simply stared, Travis grinned. "I checked. As any good friend would."

"Nick didn't find it necessary."

"Where do you think I got the idea?"

With a sigh, Spencer grabbed a towel, shooting Nick a, *are you kidding me* look. For three years, their play on the field had run like a well-oiled machine. They made up what experts called one of the best third base, shortstop, second base defensive combos in the history of the game.

Off the field, the three men spent more time with each other than anybody else. From wild parties to even wilder vacations, to a quiet drink and some video games.

Yet, no matter how well Spencer knew them, every now and then they surprised the hell out of him.

"I don't know why you're suddenly pushing me toward a woman. But listen close. Knock it off."

Nick waited until Spencer was well out of earshot before turning to Travis.

"Is he really that deep in denial? We aren't pushing him toward any woman."

"Spencer knows." Chuckling, Travis shook his head, a bit of

the southern accent he's dropped long ago coming through. "Jesus. I never imagined when I was growing up in shit poor rural South Carolina that I'd ever play Cupid."

"I hear you, brother. We were too busy worrying about finding our next meal. Cupid wouldn't have survived five minutes in my old neighborhood. Roasted. Fried. Wouldn't have mattered."

Nick could laugh now. When he was a kid in Los Angeles, and so hungry it felt like his stomach was eating away at itself, he hadn't found the humor in much of anything.

"We're latent romantics, my friend." Travis looked pleased with the idea. "I never believed in happily ever after. I'm not sure that's changed. But if anybody deserves one, it's Spencer."

"DINNER. WHAT CAN it hurt?"

Blue gritted her teeth, slowly counting to ten. What was it about muscle-headed jocks? The word no—at least when it came to women—seemed to vanish from their vocabularies at an early age.

And why, oh why, did most men believe—from athlete to ditch digger—that any woman alone at a bar was fair game?

Technically, Blue wasn't alone. Or, she wouldn't be as soon as Ross Burton, his wife Sherry, and their two teenage sons arrived.

Ross, the Cyclones' majority owner, was in Arizona to check out the team. Like Blue, this was the first of several visits during the month of Spring Training games. This time, he brought his family along.

However, Jock Pontiac didn't know that when he approached Blue in the lounge of the Ramada Inn. Nor was he open to listening to her explanation when she politely tried to tell him that she was waiting for friends.

Blue found one consolation. The paunchy pitcher played for a different team. If he were a member of the Cyclones, she'd feel obligated to don a cloak of diplomacy.

Because of her position, Blue understood she couldn't cause a scene. No shouting. No slap across the face. No knee to the groin. Not that she wasn't tempted. Especially when his big paw landed on her leg.

Blue's gaze turned from annoyed to icy. The jerk was pushing his luck. Her father made certain his children knew how to take care of themselves. Foolishly, he touched her with his multi-million-dollar pitching hand.

Though Blue had never used the move, she'd practiced it often enough. Little did the big galoot know that he was a whim away from a season-ending broken finger. Snap. Jock Pontiac spends six months riding the bench.

Luckily, Blue wasn't a violent person. And she'd never risk her job in such a ridiculous manner.

However, nothing stopped Blue from quietly using her wits to knock the jerk down a peg or two. Gently but firm to start. If he didn't get the point, she'd harden her approach. She might enjoy that.

It had been awhile since Blue had verbally eviscerated anybody.

"Want to play a game?"

Silly question. The way she asked. The husky quality of her voice. If Jock had said no, Blue would've fallen off the stool.

"Sure," he leaned closer.

The overwhelming scent of Jock's cologne made Blue wrinkle her nose. She blinked, certain the fumes made her eyes sting.

"Close your eyes."

Proving he wasn't a complete fool, Jock hesitated. Proving he was a man when Blue turned on her most winning smile, he did exactly as she asked.

"Picture this. You enter the bar. Any bar. Sitting on one of the stools is a young woman. She's enjoying a drink. Not bothering anybody. Minding her own business."

"Sounds good," Jock said, his grin cocky.

"But it isn't just any woman."

"No?" Getting into the game, Jock's smile widened.

"It's one of your sisters."

"What?" Jock's eyes popped open. From the wariness in his dark brown eyes, she could tell he didn't like where this was headed. "Why?"

"Because, Jock. I'm somebody's sister. Somebody's daughter. Even if I weren't, I should have the right to sit here without getting hit on." Jock still looked confused, though Blue thought there might be a bit of a light dawning. "You asked. I turned you down. That should've ended it."

"I thought you were playing hard to get."

"Pretend I'm your sister, Jock. Would you accept that excuse from a guy who wouldn't take no for an answer?"

Jock shook his head, rubbing the back of his neck. "I'd punch the guy's teeth down his throat," he grumbled.

Blue felt a burst of satisfaction. Maybe—just maybe—she'd succeeded in the re-education of Jock Pontiac. Or, tomorrow night, he might enter this same bar and forget what he learned. Either way, Blue's message had been received loud and clear.

Out of the corner of Blue's eye, she caught sight of a man moving her way. Spencer. Just her luck. Tall. Dark. Casually dressed in jeans and a light blue button-down shirt. As always, he looked like a million bucks.

Blue wanted to wave him off. But he only looked her way for an instant. His gaze was locked on Jock.

"Hello, Jock."

Spencer held out his hand. Seemingly a friendly gesture, the way he stood near to Blue—hovering, but not quite touching her arm—sent an entirely different message. He exuded an air of protectiveness—bordering on possessiveness—that Blue neither wanted nor appreciated.

"Spence."

Though Jock was several inches taller and weighed at least sixty pounds more, next to Spencer—all lean, chiseled granite—he looked more like an unformed pile of molding clay.

"You look beautiful tonight, Blue. But then, you always do."

"You two know each other?"

Jock sent Blue an accusatory look as if she'd deliberately withheld this vital piece of information. She rolled her eyes. How did men dare call women illogical? Did they ever stop and listen to themselves?

"Blue and I've known each other... How long has it been?"

Spencer frowned as if he honestly couldn't remember.

"Almost twenty years."

"That's right." Tilting his head, Spencer smiled. "You have a birthday coming up fast. April ninth."

When they were dating, Spencer never forgot her birthday. He had a way of making them special. Not with big, elaborate parties or expensive gifts. A simple rose. A drive in the country and a picnic.

A kiss that scrambled her brains so much, she missed the moment Spencer fastened a necklace around her neck. Blue wore the platinum chain with the dangling sapphire-shaped bluebell every day. Never taking it off until…

Without thinking, Blue's hand went to her neck, finding it bare. Spencer's gaze followed, drifting up, meeting hers. Her breath caught in her throat. No matter how she tried, she could never escape their shared memories. There were too many. Most of them damn good.

"I guess I'll be going." Jock sent Spencer an annoyed look. Blue received a slight smile. "Maybe another time? All that red hair. I can't wait to find out if it's natural."

"Watch your mouth, Pontiac," Spencer warned.

Alertly, Blue slid from the barstool, placing herself between them. She wished she had the power to send them to their rooms for a timeout. What worked with her three-year-old niece didn't have the same effect on grown men. More's the pity.

"Jock," Blue placed a hand on the pitcher's arm. "Remember your sister."

"My sister wouldn't be hanging out alone in a bar."

Jock stomped away, his big, boot-covered feet shaking the beer bottles on a nearby table.

"Okay," Blue said with a shrug. "I guess the *bitch* was implied."

"I don't know Jock well. Though the one time I faced him during a game, he plunked me pretty good." Spencer rubbed his shoulder. "The bruise was a thing of beauty. What was that thing about his sister?"

"My misguided attempt to do the impossible."

Reprogramming didn't happen in an instant. However, Blue had planted the seed. Perhaps it would grow. Perhaps Jock would morph into a more sensitive individual.

More likely, he'd continue with his Neanderthal, knuckle-dragging ways. Either way, she wouldn't spend any time worrying about it.

"I meant what I said."

Eyebrows raised, Blue focused her attention on Spencer.

"Is that something new? Do I have to filter through our past conversations wondering when you *didn't* mean what you said?"

"A less-evolved man would accuse you of being a ball buster." Spencer laughed as he said the words.

"But not you." Blue's lips twitched in spite of herself.

Spencer leaned against the bar, physically moving a few feet away. However, his emerald gaze felt like a warm, gentle caress across Blue's skin.

"I like a strong-minded woman. I like *you*. Always have. Sharp tongue. Sharp wit. Only a fool would have a problem with either."

Whoa. Blue's stomach did a slow roll. She hadn't forgotten what it felt like to be the center of Spencer's attention. Still, it had been four years. Time enough—she'd hoped—to become immune.

Blue sighed. Apparently, once hooked on Spencer Kraig, getting him completely out of her blood was impossible. A month ago, that would have distressed her. Now...? She didn't have an answer.

Lord knew Blue had looked hard to find a substitute. Unfortunately, nothing compared. Not even close.

"Spencer—"

Whatever Blue had been about to say was cut off by the arrival of Ross Burton and his wife.

A big man both regarding the size of his body and his personality, the owner of the Cyclones filled up a room the second he entered. Tall and close to three hundred pounds, he looked like a vacationing Santa Claus—substituting his red suit for a tan and casual attire.

However, anybody foolish enough to believe Ross' jovial demeanor meant he was a pushover when it came to business quickly learned their mistake. Before jumping into the world of professional baseball, he cut his teeth in corporate America. And made a fortune in the process.

Most of the time, Ross treated his players as a part of the family. But when the time came, he could be a stern, no-nonsense parent. Money was the bottom line. Winning followed closely behind. If you no longer cut it with the Cyclones, he wouldn't hesitate to send you packing. Either to another team or in some cases, into oblivion.

Professional sports was a cutthroat business. For a good reason, some people—out of earshot—called round-cheeked, perpetually smiling Ross Burton *the executioner*.

As Tom Hanks once famously said, there's no crying in baseball. Nor was there room for sentimentality. When deadwood needed eliminating, Ross took care of it.

Quick, clean, and painlessly as possible.

"I didn't expect to see you here." The Cyclones' owner looked pleased. He held out his hand. "Good to see you, Spencer."

"Hello, Ross. And your beautiful wife," Spencer smiled at Sherry Burton. "Are you enjoying the Arizona sunshine?"

As thin as her husband was wide, Sherry Burton's personality matched Ross' perfectly. The attractive brunette bubbled with warmth and personality.

"What do you think? Yesterday, I shivered through my morning coffee. Today, the boys and I spent the day by the pool." Sherry sighed with happiness, her dark eyes sparkling. "I love Spring Training."

"How do you feel about it, Blue? Are you enjoying your first foray into spring baseball?"

"This is my first time in a professional capacity," Blue informed Ross. "But I've been before."

"Really?" Ross raised his bushy dark eyebrows. "Sounds like a story I want to hear. Our table is ready. Let's continue this conversation in the dining room. Spencer? Will you join us?"

Blue sent Spencer a look that said, *don't you dare*. A look that Spencer chose to ignore.

"Thank you, Ross. I'd love to."

Spencer's smile encompassed the group, but his eyes lingered on Blue. He made a gesture with his hand, indicating she should precede him. She held back until Ross and Sherry were far enough ahead of them so her words wouldn't be overheard.

"What are you doing?" Blue hissed

"Walking toward what I anticipate will be an excellent meal. The chef here knows her way around a piece of prime rib."

"Don't be cute."

"I—"

Knowing exactly the quip Spencer planned on making—something about he couldn't help it, he was born that way—Blue stopped him with her sharp gaze.

"You aren't *that* cute. Certainly not at the moment."

"Relax, Bluebell. This isn't a date. You aren't expected to kiss me when I walk you to your door—unless you find yourself overcome with desire. In that case, I won't complain. Or fight you off."

"Oh, for the love of—" Blue wondered at Spencer. Had he forgotten the last time they were together? "You seem awfully cocky considering how we left things."

"Not cocky. Hopeful."

Hopeful, Blue thought. The word—and all its connotations—had followed her all the way from her bedroom in Seattle to a hotel bar in Arizona.

"What exactly are you hoping for?"

Blue held her breath. Part of her wanted to hear Spencer's answer. The other part…? Who was she kidding? Every bit of her wanted to know what he was thinking.

Too bad the trip from the bar to the dining room was a short one. They arrived before Spencer could enlighten her. However, as he held her chair for her to sit, he whispered.

"I'll tell you later. If you're still interested."

Silly question. Blue was only human. Of course, she was interested. And from the light in his eyes, Spencer knew it.

Damn the man.

"This is one of my favorite hotels. Bar none." Ross adjusted his sizable girth, getting as close to the table as his stomach would allow. "The rooms are comfortable. The service top-notch. And the food." He laughed—mostly at himself—patting his belly. "Our boys have their father's appetite. Luckily, they inherited their mother's metabolism."

"I left Ross Jr. and Tristan by the pool," Sherry said, explaining why the younger Burtons weren't with them. "They preferred another hour of swimming and room service to, and I quote, *boring, grown-up talk.* Though if they'd known Spencer would be here, they undoubtedly would've changed their tune."

"They're fine young men." Spencer smiled at the proud parents.

"That they are," Ross said with a nod.

After they'd ordered, Sherry turned to Blue.

"Please continue what you were saying in the bar. How this isn't your first Spring Training?"

"My dad taught me everything I know about baseball." Blue watched as the waitress delivered her glass of white wine, thanking her. "Lauren and Dale, my brother and sister, like the game, I adore it. For Christmas one year, my gift was a trip to Arizona to watch the Cyclones. A whole week. Just me and my father."

"How lovely," Sherry beamed. "We always hear stories about fathers and sons bonding over baseball. Yours is the first I've heard about a father and daughter."

"You'd be surprised how often it happens. For Dad, baseball is a passion. When my brother didn't share his feelings, I know he was disappointed. Luckily, I made up for Dale's disinterest."

"Lucky for both you *and* your father."

Though Blue rarely thought about how fortunate she was, that didn't mean she took her parents—their love and support—for granted.

Baseball was a perfect example.

Blue's father wanted somebody to share his love of the venerable game. He had no preference. Son or daughter. And her mother had been happy to watch her husband bond so tightly with his little girl.

Happy. That word summed up the O'Hara clan. Not perfect—thank God. How boring would that be? Blue loved each member of her family. Warts and all.

Her parents had raised three fairly well-adjusted individuals who contributed to society. They taught Blue and her siblings well. Love thy neighbor—but never let them walk all over you. Stand up for what's right. Help those less fortunate. If help isn't possible, do no harm.

Neither saints nor sinners, Blue's family fell somewhere wonderfully in between.

"Blue is an unusual name," Ross took a sip of his wine, smiling. "What's the origin?"

Blue understood when Ross invited her to dinner, the purpose was to get to know her. Smart. Exactly what she'd have done. A wise leader kept his eyes straight ahead, while never losing sight of his soldiers. To succeed—no, to flourish—he made a point to discover their strengths and weaknesses. He never knew when the knowledge would come in handy.

At the moment, Blue wasn't high on the Cyclones' food chain. But one day, she might be. Ross seemed jovial. Relaxed.

Underneath, she understood that much more was happening.

An informal future job interview—for want of a better description.

Blue's path was clear. One day, she'd head the PR department. However, the final decision wasn't hers to make. Ross didn't have to like her—though that wouldn't hurt. He *did* have to trust her.

A little thing like how Blue's parents came up with her name might have seemed like a benign question. The point wasn't her answer. This was a step. Small, but heading in the right direction.

"Originally, Dad wanted to call me Beatrice—after his mother."

"You don't look like a Bea," Sherry observed. With her fork, she speared an olive from the salad, waving it for emphasis. "Blue suits you much better."

"I agree. Luckily, Mom pulled the, *I just survived twelve hours of labor card.*"

"A card I'm well acquainted with." Taking Sherry's hand, Ross squeezed, his eyes filled with warm affection.

Blue smiled. She grew up around openly affectionate parents. Cynicism was easy in this day and age of celebrity insta-couples. In love one second, out the next. However, she could testify that the real deal existed. Connie and Clark O'Hara were her shining example.

Unless Blue's radar was out of whack, she could add Ross and

Sherry to that small, but encouraging, list.

"Understandably, Mom was still a little groggy when, back in her hospital room, she held me. Dad sat on the edge of the bed. Beaming proudly. According to Mom, when she looked up, she was struck by the mid-afternoon sky. Crystal clear. Dazzlingly blue."

"Ah," Sherry nodded. "Inspiration struck *out of the blue*."

Ross groaned. "Bet you've never heard that one before."

"Once or twice," Blue laughed with good humor. "The important part? Dad didn't have the heart to argue. Beatrice was out. Blue was in."

"I think the name is lovely. But as I said, unusual. Children can be cruel. Sometimes unintentionally. Were you teased?"

Without conscious thought, Blue's eyes fell on Spencer.

Spencer's gaze holding hers. She was certain his lips twitched. "Cruelty was never my intention."

"You and Spencer have known each other a long time, haven't you?" Sherry leaned in with interest. "Didn't you date for a while?"

"Sherry…" Ross warned his wife.

"I'm sorry. Was that rude? You seem so at ease with each other." Sherry seemed genuinely contrite. With a sigh, she said, "Hello. My name is Sherry, and I'm a gossip addict."

"Hello, Sherry." Laughing, Blue shook Sherry's outstretched hand. "I can't speak for Spencer. But I don't think this is technically considered gossip."

Spencer sent Sherry an automatic, unintentionally sigh-inducing smile. Right on cue, she heard a gasp of air escape the woman's mouth.

"Blue's right. Our past relationship is common knowledge. Yes, we dated."

"And...?" It seemed Sherry couldn't help herself. "Any chance we see a reconciliation?"

"Sherry!" Ross' voice lost its indulgent tone. "That is none of your business." He looked first at Blue, then Spencer. "To put a cap on this conversation, let me be clear. The Cyclones have no objection to our employees dating. However. If it were to become a distraction, that rule could change. Very quickly."

Blue didn't know what to say. The turn of events had her flummoxed.

Running the exchange through her head, she couldn't for the life of her figure out when she'd indicated the slightest desire to resume her relationship with Spencer.

Yet for some reason, Ross felt compelled to give them the green light. With a very important proviso.

They had Ross' blessing. Unless things become messy. Then every woman for herself. Make no mistake. Blue was expendable. Spencer wasn't.

Warning given and received.

When it came to Spencer, Blue didn't know what she wanted. She was fairly certain he felt the same about her. The waters had cleared—slightly. But not enough.

When it came to Blue's career, she had no doubts. She knew exactly what she wanted and how to get it.

Blue was no longer a starry-eyed young woman with a vague and endless future stretching out as far as the eye could see. Which meant, if anything—*anything*—happened between her and Spencer, she had to be certain the risk was worth taking.

This time more than Blue's heart was at stake.

CHAPTER ELEVEN

"WALKING ME TO my room wasn't necessary."

Spencer shrugged. "For my peace of mind, indulge me."

As Blue retrieved the keycard from her purse, she couldn't help but dwell on how she felt finding Spencer at her side.

The way he automatically shortened his stride to meet hers. How his arm almost brushed hers. How she wished it would.

Normal and right versus unnerving and unsettling.

The battle warred inside Blue. Deep down, she knew which side she wanted to win. But she had to ask herself. Was she rooting for good or evil?

"Want to share the joke?"

Realizing she hadn't kept her laughter to herself, Blue shook her head.

"Crazy thoughts. Nothing worth repeating."

As they reached her door, Spencer shot Blue a skeptical look.

"Something tells me you're not telling me everything. But I'll let it slide."

"Gee. Thanks." Sarcasm dripped from each word. "FYI? I didn't give you a choice."

"I could badger you."

"I could slam the door in your face."

"Or," Spencer said, his hand shooting out to prevent Blue from doing exactly that. "You could invite me in."

"No. I couldn't."

Blue's gaze was steady. Her tone, emphatic. Spencer didn't need to know that temptation sat on her shoulder, whispering in her ear.

Where's the harm?

"Just for a little while?"

Spencer didn't whisper. But he was plenty tempting.

Blue couldn't help remember when she'd used similar words to coax him into having sex with her for the first time. From the slow smile that formed on his lips, Spencer's thoughts were headed the same way as hers.

"What do you want, Spencer?"

"Something to drink?"

"Don't play the fool," Blue said, her patience wearing thin. "You know what I meant. Us. What do you want to happen?"

"I don't know. But—"

"No buts, Spencer. No ifs. No ands. I need a straight out, to the point, bullshit-free answer."

"Fair enough." Heaving a sigh, Spencer ran a hand through his hair. "How about you, Blue? What do you want?"

"I don't know. Not that long ago I thought I did."

Funny, Blue thought. Suddenly, not so long ago felt like years.

"On that, we can agree."

Blue found a little solace in the fact that Spencer looked as confused as she felt. The normally clear green of his irises was shadowed with emotions she recognized all too well.

Conflict. With a chaser of doubt.

"Falling into bed with each other would be easy."

Spencer nodded, desire flaring in his eyes.

"I want more. However," Blue hurried, not ready for Spencer's answer. If he had one. "I don't know if I want more with you."

"Is there a chance for me?" Spencer's gaze sharpened as if the possibility appealed to him. "A chance for us?"

"That's the sixty-four-thousand-dollar question."

Without another word—she had nothing else to say—Blue entered her hotel room and slowly closed the door. But before she could click it shut, Spencer stopped her.

"I changed my mind," he said.

"You can't come in, Spencer." Blue planted her feet, determined to keep him out. The spiked heels of her shoes didn't give her a lot of support, but they wouldn't stop her from trying.

"That's not what I meant." Spencer held the edge of the door in a white-knuckled grip. "I don't know if breaking up with you was the right decision. But I sure as hell know the way I went about it turned into a fucking disaster."

Blue couldn't argue. Her legs feeling a little wobbly, she crossed her arms, waiting for Spencer to continue.

"I don't want to make an even bigger mistake by not telling you how I feel."

"Okay."

"I don't know if I deserve another chance. But if you can find it in your heart to give me one, I'll jump at it. Both feet. No hesitation."

Blue took a shaky breath. Too soon, part of her cried. The cautious part that still remembered the pain. The other part. Reckless with a shorter memory wanted to grab Spencer and damn the consequences.

As if sensing her struggle, Spencer backed off.

"Whatever you need. However long it takes. I'm in, Blue. All the way. Call me. Text me. Send up smoke signals. I'll be there."

Closing the door, Blue sank onto the bed, her heart racing. She had a lot to consider. But at the moment, two words kept circling through her mind on a constant, giddy loop.

Holy crap.

THE CYCLONES' CHARITY golf tournament was an annual event. One day out of their usual Spring Training routine, the players looked forward to it. Fans lined the course for a chance to see some of their favorite athletes out of the usual venue.

A good cause and plenty of fun. The event was a no-brainer regarding turnout and success.

Blue could've run the PR side blindfolded with one hand tied behind her back. Her presence wasn't necessary. A safety measure just in case.

Whatever *just in case* was, it never happened. Not in the history of the event. And not today. As a result, Blue was able to enjoy the beautiful, cloudless Arizona afternoon.

Officially, on the job. But with nothing to do but bask in the sun, Blue's mind naturally wandered to more personal thoughts.

On the edge of the golf course, surrounded by excited spectators, flanked by her boss' wife and two sons, all Blue could think about was Spencer. And the words he left her with the night before.

I'm in, Blue. All the way.

Whatever you need. However long it takes.

Call me. Text me. Send up smoke signals. I'll be there.

Unexpected. Shocking. Thrilling. Spencer's declaration had quite literally taken Blue's breath away. She had to remind herself to breathe. Sitting on the bed, her hands clutching the covers, her mind spinning, she took in much-needed oxygen while wondering if her heart raced out of excitement, fear, or a crazy combination of the two.

Blue's sleep—what there was of it—was filled with Spencer.

Her first waking thought? *Spencer.* As she showered? Picked out the perfect outfit—yellow Capri pants, sleeveless white shirt, and flat, strappy sandals perfect for walking on a golf course? Checked her messages?

Spencer, Spencer, Spencer.

If the man's motive had been to invade her mind to the exclusion of all else, mission accomplished.

"I'm not a big golf fan," Sherry Burton said. Dressed for the warm day, she wore crisp white Bermuda shorts and a floral top. She removed her big, floppy hat, using it as a fan before returning it to her head. "But I do enjoy watching well-built young men in motion. Very nice."

Blue couldn't argue. The object of Sherry's attention was the Cyclones' buzzed-about rookie outfielder Drake Langford, as he stepped up to take his turn, driver in hand.

Young, tall, blond, muscular, Langford looked as if he'd just stepped off a box of Wheaties.

The perfect all-American boy. It didn't hurt that he could hit a nasty slider over the center field fence. Or track a fly ball like a state-of-the-art GPS unit.

"There's already talk of him winning rookie of the year. What do you think?"

"That March is the time for hyperbole," Blue observed. "Let's talk again in September."

Sherry laughed. "I always know when I'm talking to a true baseball person. Like my husband, you won't be drawn into making predictions."

"That isn't true. I predict today will be a smashing success."

"That's like saying the sun will come up in the east."

"I only bet on sure things." Smiling, Blue adjusted her sunglasses. "However, I'll concede that Drake Langford has the potential to be a superstar. Five-tool players are hard to come by. The Cyclones are lucky to have him."

"Five tools?" Sherry sighed. "Ross would bust a gasket if I admitted how little I know about this game and all the terms."

"Hitting for power and average, fielding ability, throwing ability, and speed."

"Spencer!" Delighted, Sherry put a hand on his arm. "How lucky am I? I ask a question, and a handsome young man materializes to answer."

Unconcerned by the stir his presence caused around them, Spencer patted Sherry's hand.

"When I noticed the beautiful woman in the gallery, I couldn't resist coming over."

"Such a charmer."

Blue was a firm believer in the idea that no woman over a certain age should giggle. Period. She made no exceptions.

Yet, for some unfathomable reason, Sherry Burton managed to pull the sound off with perfect aplomb.

Spencer turned toward Blue. Dressed for a day on the links, his long legs were encased in a pair of casual khakis. Black golf shoes. The short-sleeved polo shirt of the same color showed off his tanned, muscular arms to perfection.

The dark sunglasses made it impossible for Blue to see his eyes. But she had no problem picturing them

Emerald green. Bright as a newly mown meadow. Focused intently on Blue.

"Hello."

One word and her heart beat faster.

"Spencer."

Blue wasn't in danger of giggling. Between the arid, desert air, and an inconveniently sudden case of nerves, she was lucky to push Spencer's name past her dry tongue and parched lips.

Thank goodness Sherry's sons had no such problem. Not quite teenagers, Ross Jr. and Tristan pounced on Spencer with enviable ease, breaking the tension.

"Are you going to hit forty homers this year, Spencer?" Tristan asked, his dark hair gleaming with streaks.

"More like fifty," Ross Jr. proclaimed with the superiority of an older—and therefore, much wiser—brother.

The golfers had moved to the next hole, so his mother saw no need to tamp down on the boys' ramped-up exuberance.

"We'll see," Spencer chuckled, placing a friendly hand on Ross Jr.'s shoulder, repeating the gesture with Tristan.

Basking in Spencer's attention, the Burton brothers seemed to grow several inches, their necks bent as they gazed at their idol with wide-eyed adoration.

"Individual stats are great. But baseball is a team sport. If I hit one or one hundred homers," Spencer winked. The boys snickered. "All that matters is helping the Cyclones win. Am I right?"

Tristan and Ross Jr. nodded, on board with anything Spencer had to say. Thank goodness he used his powers for good, Blue thought with a smile. In the wrong hands, the kind of blind devotion he inspired could wreak unimaginable havoc.

"Good kids," Spencer said as Sherry hustled the reluctant boys along, anxious not to miss Ross Sr. tee off.

Taking a water bottle from her bag, Blue nodded. She swallowed half the contents before replacing the cap.

"Aren't you playing?" she asked, relieved her words came out fairly normal instead of a dry, raspy croak.

"I'll catch up."

Reaching out, Spencer took the water from Blue's hand. Removing the cap, he raised the bottle to his lips, emptying what remained. The gesture felt so... intimate. His mouth where hers had been just moments earlier.

Shared fluids. The implication was undeniably sexual.

Spencer tossed the bottle into a nearby garbage can.

"Is this an awkward silence?" Spencer asked.

"Maybe." Blue thought for a second. "Probably.

"Must be a first for us." With a frown, Spencer rubbed the back of his neck. "Because of what I said last night?"

"You surprised me," Blue admitted. To put it mildly.

Spencer lifted his hand as if he wanted to touch her. At the last moment, he clenched his fist, dropping it to his side.

"I meant every word, Blue." Spencer lowered his glasses. Peering over the edge, the expression in his eyes was pensive. "Too soon?"

"You want the truth?"

"From you? Always."

Blue looked around. They weren't drawing any attention. Yet. But the longer they continued such a personal conversation in such a public place, somebody was bound to eventually take notice.

"You go that way," Blue pointed toward the south entrance of the club house. "I'll go around back. There's an empty conference room near the registration desk. Meet me there."

"How do you know? About the room? Or whether or not it's empty?"

"I arranged for a tour of the facilities before anybody else arrived."

When Spencer raised an inquiring eyebrow, Blue shrugged.

"Be prepared. That motto doesn't just apply to the Scouts."

Without another word, Blue casually, but with purpose, strolled along the path leading to the clubhouse. Glancing over her shoulder, she saw Spencer doing the same.

As subterfuge went, her plan was pretty lame. However, Blue wasn't on anybody's radar. The crowd came to see celebrity baseball players. Not the assistant to the head of Cyclones' PR.

Spencer would draw eyes. The ultra-famous always did. And when that person had the face of a slightly fallen angel—and the body to match? Anonymity was impossible.

However, Spencer knew how to slip away when he wanted some privacy. Blue had seen his skills at work—back in the day. She had no worry that he'd make their rendezvous without attracting a crowd.

As Blue expected, the clubhouse was almost deserted. She passed a few staff members going about their business, but for the most part, everybody was where they were supposed to be.

Out on the golf course.

Slightly out of breath—with anticipation—Blue slipped into the conference room.

"What took you so long?"

Blue jumped, her hand grasping her chest as if worried that if she didn't, her heart would jump free.

"Me?" she exclaimed to a smirking Spencer. "How did you get here so fast?"

The route she took was shorter, Blue knew that for a fact.

Spencer appeared relaxed. He leaned against a chair-lined table, long legs stretched out, ankles crossed. "You forget, Bluebell. This isn't my first trip to this facility. I scoped out the shortcuts long ago."

"Why?" In spite of herself, Blue couldn't resist asking. Then, wisely, she decided she didn't want to know. "Never mind."

Reading her perfectly, Spencer chuckled. "Nothing sexual."

"No longer my business." The last thing Blue wanted was a rundown—slim or detailed—concerning Spencer's sex life.

"No," he agreed. Standing, Spencer's gaze sharpened. "But that brings us to the question on the table. Do you want my sex life— my *whole* life—to become your business again?"

Wow. Blue had to hand it to Spencer. He wasn't afraid to speak his mind. Or tell her what he wanted. First last night. Now this afternoon. She wasn't there yet.

"Do you still hate me, Blue?"

The question brought Blue up short. Made her think. Finding an answer didn't take long.

"I hate the way you ended our relationship. Always will."

Spencer's green eyes clouded over. Pain. Blue understood the feeling. At one time, she wanted him to hurt the way she did. But not anymore. The revelation lightened her spirit considerably.

"I don't hate *you*, Spencer. Lord knows I tried. I convinced myself that I did."

Blue couldn't count how many times she said those very words to Jordyn. I hate Spencer. Jordyn's response? Every time? No, you don't.

Funny thing about a best friend. Often, she understands you better than you understand yourself.

"Oh, Blue. You have no idea how relieved I am to hear that." Spencer's smile wasn't a full-on grin. Close. But not quite. "Have dinner with me."

"I can't."

"You have to eat."

"True." Blue loved to eat. "And I'd say yes. Unfortunately, there's a flight leaving for Seattle in three hours, and I have to be on it."

"What is with your boss?" Spencer sounded as disappointed as Blue felt. A fact that gave her ego a nice boost. "What kind of crazy patchwork plane connections does he have you making this time?"

"I learned my lesson. Unless Vance catches me off guard, I make my own travel arrangements. Non-stop whenever possible."

"That's something." Spencer moved closer until he stood a foot away. "When will you be back?"

Originally, three trips to Arizona were penciled in on Blue's schedule. A press day and a dinner for a local orphanage. That had changed late last week when Vance suddenly decided to go in her place.

Though he didn't give a reason, Blue had her suspicions. She made the mistake of appearing too eager to carry out her assignment. Vance had a petty streak a mile wide and wasn't shy about showing it.

"Bastard," Spencer growled.

More and more, Blue felt a sharpening edge to Vance's animosity that seemed to go beyond simple jealousy or dislike.

"I bring out the worst in him."

"You're young, ambitious, and on the rise. Your boss is none of those things. Some people handle the backend of their career with grace. Then there are the Vance Sutters of the world. Because they have nothing else, they get their jollies by spraying their bitterness over everybody else."

Vance could spew a vat of bitterness Blue's way. She wouldn't let him mess with her head. However, if he tried something else? Something personal? He'd soon find out that if he messed with her, she wasn't afraid to hit back. Hard.

"We need to get back," Blue said. "We have responsibilities we're shirking."

"One more thing. May I call you?"

"Of course." Spencer looked so earnest, Blue had to bite the inside of her lip to keep from smiling.

"Every day?"

"If you like."

A pleasant warmth spread through Blue. The heat she felt was reflected in Spencer's eyes.

"I do like. Very much." Spencer hesitated. A rare occurrence for a man with his confidence. "I want to hug you. But…"

"The road back has shortened considerably." Miles melted with every passing day. "I'm not ready for a lot of things. But it isn't too soon for this."

Blue wrapped her arms around Spencer, pressing her lips to his. He pulled her close, molding her body to his—without an ounce of hesitation.

The kiss wasn't what she'd expected. They didn't fumble, awkwardly trying to figure what had changed and how to make this work.

They came together so naturally, Blue sighed with wonder. This—Spencer's touch—is what she'd missed with other men. They… fit. She couldn't think of a better way to describe the feeling. After a second, she couldn't think at all.

Making up for four years with one kiss was impossible. But they tried. Blue's toes curled—actually, physically curled as Spencer's tongue touched hers. Her legs grew weak, but Spencer's strong arms were there, holding her tight.

Thoughts swirling on a tide of bliss, Blue wondered how she survived for so long without the taste of him. Oh, yes, she sighed.

Like nobody else. So sweet. So hot.

So… Spencer.

"When do you have to leave," Spencer asked, his chest rising and falling, his breathing hard

"Soon."

Blue gasped as Spencer's teeth grazed the vein that pulsed wildly along the side of her neck.

Reluctantly—torturously—she pushed at his arms. Slowly, Spencer complied, dropping his hold. Blue's emotions warred. Gratitude or regret. Neither could win—not yet—the battle ending in a virtual tie.

"Too soon," she said.

"I won't push."

Though Spencer looked as if it took all his willpower not to do just that. And Blue wasn't sure—if he gave in to his desires—that she'd have the strength to say no.

"If you like, we can have dinner as soon as you get back to Seattle."

"April third. The season opens the next day."

Spencer's lips quirked. Blue smiled. They both knew what that meant. An early night—and no sex.

"I'll cook."

"The hell you say?" Spencer scoffed. His response effectively broke the tension. "When did you learn to do more than boil water?"

"I always could," Blue insisted. In her book, toast and scrambled eggs counted.

Spencer sent her a skeptical look.

"Fine. I'll order out."

"Sounds like a plan." Taking her hand, Spencer raised it to his lips. His kiss lingered. Soft, but filled with promise.

Blue felt a rush of emotions. Anticipation. Hope—her current favorite. And a myriad of others that were too complicated to sort through.

Maybe she and Spencer would get it right this time. Maybe not. But either way, the doubt was gone.

Succeed or fail. Blue knew she'd never be happy unless she tried.

CHAPTER TWELVE

MARCH DREW TO a close with the Cyclones in good shape both physically and mentally. The closer the team inched toward the start of the season, the antsier the players became.

Restlessness was normal. Spencer would've worried if he and his teammates *weren't* chomping at the proverbial bit.

Spring Training served an important purpose. Knocking off the cobwebs. Honing their skills. Building chemistry. But by the third week, practice games became more of a necessary evil.

When the Cyclones broke camp on April third, to a man, they swore if they never saw the training facilities again, it would be too soon. Of course, next year—around the middle of January—that would change. Again.

Playing baseball—playing *any* sport—was a cycle. Love of the game—and a blissfully short memory—made every season feel brand new.

Spencer never had a problem getting geared up for the season. This would be his eighth campaign—Jesus, where had the time gone? He understood the ebbs and flows.

The quote *hope springs eternal* wasn't coined with baseball in mind. But when referencing the game, the words were prophetic.

Each year began with nothing but high expectations. Even the teams with no real shot at a winning record harbored not-so-silent dreams of playing meaningful September baseball.

Then there was the handful of organizations—like the Cyclones—with a real chance. Surprises happened. That one team that miraculously came out of nowhere to challenge the norm.

Cinderella accepting her glass slipper. Or World Series trophy. Then the unimaginable happened, the sports world cheered. Miracles were good for the game.

However, most of the time, the front-runners were the ones to cross the finish line. That's simply the way games—and life— worked.

Was it fair? If asked, Spencer's answer was always an emphatic *hell, yes*!

Money and smart draft picks could give a team certain advantages. But nothing could make the players deliver.

Desire. Determination. Want. Need.

Call it what you wanted. Each person had to figure out what drove them. But when twenty-six men worked their asses off toward one goal, the results could be a thing of beauty.

Spencer knew what winning felt like. He also knew the disappointment of getting so close to the top of the mountain only to watch things crumble at the last moment. Bitter didn't begin to describe the taste left in his mouth.

The Seattle Cyclones entered the new season propelled by last year's failure. Game one of one-hundred and sixty-two would be played on their home field. The crowd would be filled with hope. Was this finally their time? Would they hoist the trophy come October?

If asked—and he was. Often. Spencer's answer was emphatic.

Hell, yes!

The bounce in Spencer's step as he entered Blue's building had as much to do with her as baseball. Though she spent the last few weeks in Seattle while he toiled away in Arizona, they made progress in rebuilding their relationship.

Texts. Emails. Phone calls. And the, *what did we do before it was invented* Facetime all contributed. Blue's open mind—her willingness to give him a second chance—did the rest.

"Good evening, Mr. Kraig." Looking up from her seat behind the front desk, Rhonda smiled. "Ms. O'Hara let me know you were coming. Go right up."

Entering the elevator, Spencer waited, the short trip seeming to take longer than he remembered. Like the baseball season to come, he and Blue weren't a sure thing.

Variables had to be considered in any equation.

To be honest, Blue made Spencer more nervous than stepping up to the plate in front of sixty thousand-plus screaming, expectant fans. He knew what to expect on a baseball diamond.

After four years apart, Blue turned out to be a bit of a wild card. She'd changed. They both had. Discovering the differences was exciting. And nerve wracking.

Spencer couldn't remember the last time a woman threw him off his stride. Maybe never? Not even the first time around with Blue. Especially not the first time, he laughed—at himself.

Present day Spencer Kraig had a healthy ego. He brimmed with confidence. But four years ago, those attributes had been off the charts.

Then, his ego was alarmingly bloated. His confidence a trifle inflated. Thankfully, both attributes had trimmed down a bit to more reasonable proportions.

Blue's confidence had risen to new, appealing—and yes, sexy—heights. Her time in New York. Living on her own. Her job. Each experience added layers that Spencer couldn't wait to peel back, explore, and thoroughly enjoy.

"Finally." Blue greeted Spencer with a huge smile, opening the door before he could knock. "That elevator seemed to take a lot longer than usual."

"Great minds think alike."

Spencer started at Blue's bare feet. Her pink-tipped toenails. The loose, flowing pants and matching sleeveless top. Her full lips, sparkling eyes, and glossy red hair piled in an artfully messy bun on top of her head.

His gaze took in the tantalizing parts of Blue. Then, he took all of her into his arms.

Finally, Spencer thought, his mouth covering hers. Without realizing, he'd been on edge since the Cyclones' plane touched down at SeaTac. One taste of Blue and his muscles began to relax. In his mind, he thought he heard them let out a long, happy sigh.

"Hello to you, too." Blue breathed when Spencer reluctantly pulled back. Her cheeks were flushed with pleasure. "I'm glad you took the initiative. All I'd planned was a friendly hug. And pizza."

"Pizza sounds good. But I'm not finished with the appetizer."

"Watch it, fella. You don't want to start something you can't finish."

Letting Blue lead him away from the front door and the living room, Spencer shrugged.

"We'll finish."

Blue handed Spencer a bottle of beer. His favorite. He took a sip, pleased that she remembered.

"Not tonight. With opening day less than twenty-four hours away, the best I can offer is a drink—one bottle, no more. A couple of slices of pepperoni, olive, and green pepper. And some company."

"I gladly take all of the above. What about tomorrow? After the game?"

Blue laughed, obviously enjoying their banter as much as he was. However, Spencer didn't miss the flare of interest in her eyes.

Of all the things that had changed, he was glad to see at least one thing hadn't. The way the clear gray of her eyes turned dark and smoky with desire.

"We'll talk about it then."

Spencer knew when to push his advantage. And when he'd be smart to pull back. Blue was in the driver's seat. She controlled their speed and direction.

Most things came easily to Spencer. Even the hard work he put into his job. He enjoyed the process. So, in the end, getting where he was had been neither work nor a hardship.

Waiting for Blue wouldn't be as easy. But when she was ready—soon. Please. Spencer knew the satisfaction would be worth it.

"I've missed you."

Blue didn't remind Spencer of the fact that they'd spoken—seen each other's faces—almost every day since she left Arizona.

Spencer meant—though he hadn't realized it until now—that he missed having Blue in his life. Her friendship. Her body.

And yes—too soon or not—he missed Blue's love.

If—on occasion—Blue wasn't the smartest person in the room, she was right near the top. She didn't need Spencer to spell out what he was thinking. The look in Blue's eyes seemed to reflect what he was felt.

Spencer hoped he wasn't deluding himself. Seeing what he wanted to see.

ABOVE ANY DATE during the calendar year. Better than Christmas. Or birthdays. Or... anything. In Blue's book, nothing could compare to opening day.

Baseball was back, baby.

The smell of the peanuts, hot dogs, and anticipation filled the air.

As an added bonus, this year, Blue was officially part of the Cyclones family.

"Calm down. This is one game. One in a long, long, long season."

Blue didn't pay any attention to the gentle derision in Jordyn's tone. Her friend was on the record as not loving baseball. She loved her brother. She loved Blue. But a game where grown men hit a little ball with an oddly shaped stick? Nope.

And—she often added—the bases weren't in the shape of a diamond. Jordyn knew her gemstones and with chalk lines outlining it didn't qualify. Not by a long shot.

Eyes glued to the field, Blue didn't care how many opening days she went to, nothing—not familiarity or Jordyn's cynicism— could dim the excitement.

Football may have surpassed it in popularity, but baseball was still America's game. In Blue's heart—and, she'd bet, the hearts of almost every man, woman, and child, packed in here to cheer on the Cyclones—that would never change.

Blue's proudest moment of the day came when she personally escorted her parents to the owner's private box, introducing Clark O'Hara to Ross Burton. The pride on her father's face—the way his chest puffed out—made Blue's eyes sting, the lump in her throat making it hard to swallow.

"You go ahead," Clark told his daughter. "Your mother and I'll be fine."

Blue had no doubt. Her father was never at a loss for words in any situation. Before she was out the door, the two men were getting on like old friends.

"Don't you have more important things to do?" Vance Sutter asked, materializing from the shadows. Hoping to what? Catch Blue loafing around, chugging back a beer?

With an inward sigh, Blue took the tablet from her bag, pulling up the long to-do list. The one Vance dropped in her lap just as she left work the day before.

Most of the items were ridiculous. Even the most anal-retentive person would've questioned why she'd been tasked with carrying them out.

But—like the good, loyal soldier she was—Blue spent her first hour at the stadium carefully checking off each item, carrying them out to the best of her ability

Blue swore she'd die of boredom before she gave Vance any

opportunity to impugn her work. Biting her tongue, she stopped herself from asking why—instead of dogging her heels—he wasn't busy taking care of team business?

"Well?" Vance asked, impatiently tapping his loafer encased foot.

"As you can see," Blue handed Vance the tablet. "Most of the items are completed."

Vance didn't bother to look at the list. With a raised eyebrow, his gaze held Blue's.

"How do I know you aren't lying?"

"Excuse me?"

"All I have is your word. As far as I know, you checked off these tasks without actually doing them."

Blue felt a flush suffuse her cheeks, the heat—and her temper—rising. Never. Not once in her entire career had anybody accused her of lying. Logically, she knew Vance's purpose. Nothing had changed. He wanted to push her out. Today's antics were simply an escalation in his tactics.

Childish. The acts of a desperate, petty man.

You know better than to rise to Vance's bait, Blue told herself, taking a deep breath. *Don't react. That's what he wants. Play it cool. Be pleasant even it kills you.*

The way she felt at the moment, her lips curving into a stiff semblance of a smile, death would be preferable. Not hers.

Vance's.

"Would you like to go over everything with me? Retrace my steps? My activities?"

With each word, as Vance's scowl deepened, Blue's jaw loosened, her teeth unclenching. She hadn't won the battle. But each victory—no matter how small—added up.

Vance thought he could wear her down. *Sorry, sucker.* Not going to happen.

"There isn't time. You better hope nothing comes back to bite you in the backside."

Sorry, Vance. Won't happen.

During each stop on her crazy-assed pile of busy work, Blue made certain she exchanged words with somebody. A janitor. A vendor. An usher. She asked questions. Made herself memorable.

And because Blue understood how Vance's mind worked—wasn't that a scary revelation—she made a list of names. If he decided to check up on her, she was prepared.

"I need you to go to the airport."

"What? Now?" Blue stared at Vance as if he were speaking a foreign language. "The game is about to start."

Blue hadn't been able to keep the disappointment from her voice. Vance smiled, a gleam of satisfaction dancing across his beady eyes.

"To celebrate opening day, Mr. Burton flew in some of his old college buddies. One—Terrance Prescott—was delayed. His flight arrives in an hour. You need to pick him up."

"I was just in the owner's box. Mr. Burton didn't mention anything about his friend to me."

"Why would he?" Vance dismissed Blue's question. "You have a job. Do it. Unless you consider this assignment beneath you?"

"Not at all. May I have the information?"

As Blue jotted down the arrival time, airline, etc., she asked herself what the catch would be. Would she discover the flight had been canceled? Something Vance already knew? Had he given her the wrong details hoping she'd miss Terrance Prescott altogether?

The possibilities were too great for Blue to calculate. So, instead of trusting Vance—like that would happen—she took the time to make a few phone calls.

Yes. According to Terrance Prescott's assistant, he was due to arrive at SeaTac in less than an hour. However, he hadn't taken a commercial flight but chose to pilot himself and his family in his private jet.

The kicker? Blue's services weren't needed. Never had been.

Arrangements were made a week ago for a car to take Prescott, his wife, and their daughter to the stadium. A little late. But in plenty of time to catch the later innings.

Blue—if Vance's plan had worked—wouldn't have been as lucky. She'd have spent her day trying to track down a VIP who neither needed, nor wanted her assistance.

Standing outside the stadium, watching absently as late-arriving fans hustled through the doors, Blue wondered what she should do about Vance.

One phone call. That was all it had taken for her to figure out his game. Did he think she was a fool? Was he clueless about how the world worked in the twenty-first century?

Technology made it almost impossible to send a savvy person on a wild goose chase. Yet that was exactly what Vance tried to do. He either believed she'd blindly take him at his word—which meant he didn't have a lot of respect for her intelligence.

Or, did Vance never consider the fact that she could—and would—check the facts before rushing to do his bidding.

Honestly, Blue didn't know which scenario she found more disturbing.

"Blue!"

Immersed in her thoughts, Blue jumped when she heard her name. Looking around, she spotted a handsome young man coming her way. The clouds circling over her head—dark and stormy—lifted immediately. Her brother's smile almost always had that effect.

Delighted to see him, Blue laughed. When Dale pulled her close, she slipped her arms around him, hugging him with all her might.

"I didn't think you could make the game."

Dale ran a non-profit foundation that provided job training for underprivileged children. Blue had invited him to opening day, but he had a meeting scheduled with a potential big donor.

"The meeting moved faster than expected. Seems this game was on everybody's mind. Mort Clayton wanted to get here for the first pitch."

"And?" Blue prompted, knowing how her brother loved to drag out a good story.

"And as of next month, the Clayton grocery chain will be an official sponsor of the *Work for the Future Foundation*."

"Congratulations!" Blue exclaimed. "Do you know where Mr. Clayton's seats are located? I want to send him and his party a Cyclone Platter."

Consisting of fries, onion rings, pretzels, hamburgers, hot dogs. More things than Blue could remember. Plus, enough beer to wash everything down. The Cyclone Platter was a promotional tool management provided when hosting bigwigs.

"Wouldn't that be a misuse of your authority?"

"Only if I don't use my own money to pay for it," Blue assured her by-the-book brother. "And before you argue, I *do* receive an employee discount."

"Fine." Dale rattled off the seat locations and the number of people in the party. "Mort invited me to join them. When I explained why I couldn't—that my sister had a seat saved for me in the owner's box—I realized my mistake. Mort was so impressed, if I'd mentioned you before the meeting, his donation might have doubled."

"Little sisters have their uses."

Dale winked. "So it would seem."

Considerably lighter of spirit, Blue linked her arm through Dale's, leading him toward the entrance. When she flashed her ID, the ticket taker waved them through.

"I spoke to Dad this morning. He sounded like a little kid."

"Mom said he wanted to leave the house right after breakfast." Blue took the back way, unlocking the entrance to the service elevator. "Keeping him at home until a decent hour took all her formidable skills."

"He always was a sucker for opening day. But this year?" Dale shook his head, sending Blue a sideways look. "Clark O'Hara's little girl works for the Cyclones. I don't know what Lauren or I'll ever do that stacks up to that achievement."

"Wait until he finds out he's going to be a grandpa."

"What?" Dale's easy smile disappeared, his suddenly stormy gaze dropping to Blue's stomach. "When?"

"Not me, you idiot." Blue rolled her eyes. "Lauren. Our married sister? Remember her?"

"Right." Letting out a relieved sigh, Dale leaned against the side of the elevator. "That's great. I know she and Hal have been trying. Why am I the last to know?"

"You aren't. Lauren plans on telling Mom and Dad tomorrow night. So, keep the news to yourself."

Blue wasn't worried. Dale loved surprises and was a master of keeping information to himself.

"I don't know what I was thinking," Dale chuckled, putting an arm around Blue's shoulders. "You aren't even dating. How could you be pregnant?"

"If you have to ask, I'm not the one to tell you. Spoiler alert. The stork is a myth."

"Ha, ha. Very funny." Dale paused. "On the subject of dating."

"No." Blue knew where her brother was headed. "Not interested."

The elevator doors opened, smooth and silent. Following Blue's lead, Dale exited close behind. The corridor was deserted, the muffled sound of the nearby crowd filtering in. They walked toward the locked doors, passing stacks of empty boxes, left there by the various food vendors.

"Come on. You've been away from Seattle for some time. Let me help boost you back into the dating scene."

"Lauren already offered. As I told her, I'm fine on my own."

"But—" Dale stared at Blue's profile. "Are you seeing somebody?"

Blue didn't know how Dale managed to read her so well. According to some people, she had an excellent poker face. Her brother saw through any attempt to hide her feelings. Always had. Apparently, always would.

"Things are… new."

"Do I know him?"

"We never talk about your girlfriends."

Deflecting Dale was never that easy.

"That would be a yes," Dale declared. "Should I start throwing out names? Or, you save me the time and the aggravation by simply spilling the information?"

Brothers. Whoever thought they were a good idea had never been grilled by one. What good were secrets? At least she knew Dale would keep his mouth shut.

"Spencer."

Grabbing Blue's arms, Dale pulled her to a stop.

"Please tell me you've met a nice plumber who coincidentally happens to be named Spencer."

"I could tell you that," Blue said. "I'd be lying. But if a non-truth makes you happy, what the hell."

"Blue…" Dale took a deep breath. "Explain to me why dating the man who broke your heart is a good idea?"

"Forgiveness is good for the soul."

"Great. Forgive the overpaid pretty boy. But don't give him

another chance to hurt you."

Because she understood, Blue didn't try to lighten the situation by pointing out that—in baseball terms—Cyclones were getting their money's worth from Spencer. And more.

"I don't know what will happen, Dale."

"If the jerk hurts you, I'll shove his teeth down his throat. That's what will happen."

"Awe." Blue patted Dale's hand. "That's sweet."

Sweet because Dale meant every word. And sweet because her brother was a lot of things. Smart. Funny. Handsome. But he wasn't a fighter.

Unless Dale hired somebody else to do the dirty work, Spencer's teeth were in no danger of going anywhere—no matter how he treated Blue.

"There's nothing I can say to change your mind?"

Shaking her head, Blue pushed at the service door. After nothing but muted sounds, the buzzing voices and wild cheers hit her like a punch to her senses.

The game must be going well. Time to join the fun.

"You'll have to trust me to take care of myself. But, believe me, I love you for caring."

"I have your back." Dale tapped Blue's nose, an affectionate gesture that always brought a smile to her face.

"And I have yours."

The door to the owner's suite was closed. A guard, dressed in a dark suit, sunglasses, and a stern expression, blocked the entrance with his big, solid body.

"Is he packing?" Dale asked in jest.

"Yes," Blue answered, completely serious.

"Well, damn."

Dale wasn't a fan of guns, but he understood the world that they lived in. Billionaires like Ross Burton traveled with personal bodyguards. Bodyguards carried concealed weapons. End of story.

"Hello, Anders."

"Ms. O'Hara." The man nodded, his dark hair cut military-grade short.

"This is my brother, Dale. He's on Mr. Burton's guest list."

Double checking—a good bodyguard never took anybody's word—Anders stepped aside to let Dale pass.

"You're not coming in?"

Thinking about Vance, Blue shook her head. Chances were good her boss was inside. Blue had a good reason for not going to the airport. And she doubted Vance would be foolish enough to bring up the subject. But he'd know that his plan had failed, turning him into a bigger sourpuss than usual.

If Blue wanted to enjoy the game—which was a given—she had to get as far away from Vance Sutter as possible.

"I have a few things to take care of. And Dale? Remember?

Keep your mouth shut."

"About Lauren's secret? Or yours?"

"Both."

Blue waited until the door closed behind Dale. Thanking Anders, she started to leave, stopping when the crowd's cheers turned from excited to frenzied. Wondering what was happening, she hurried to get a look.

Down a flight of stairs, she jogged up the ramp until she stood in the center of the storm. On each side of her, fans were on their feet, eyes glued to the field.

From this distance, way up in the nosebleed section—Blue couldn't see the batter's face as he stepped to the plate. She didn't need to. Even if she hadn't glimpsed the number on his back—twenty-three—she knew him right away.

Spencer's stance was unique. At least to Blue. The way he shuffled his feet, finding just the right spot. The way he paused, staring out at the mound, before raising his bat. Daring the pitcher to try to get a ball past him

More often than not, the pitcher failed.

Game one. One hundred and sixty-one to go. Spencer would have a lot of at-bats this season. But this was the first one Blue had seen in person in over four years. That made it—the moment—special.

Holding her breath, she waited.

The pitcher made his windup. Released the ball. A second later, Spencer swung for the fences. And that is exactly where the ball ended up. Over the center field fence. Upper deck. Three rows below where Blue stood.

The crowd went crazy. A man—a total stranger—slapped Blue on the back.

"Kraig is our man," he shouted. "Worth every freaking penny."

Soaking in the unadulterated joy that abounded around her, Blue threw her head back and laughed.

CHAPTER THIRTEEN

"WE WON."

"I know. I was there."

Spencer grinned. Blue grinned right back. An arm around her waist, he backed her through the door. From the garage to the kitchen, the lighting wasn't bright enough for her to get a good look around.

The first time in his home. The one Spencer had moved into and renovated well before Blue returned to Seattle. Naturally, she was curious.

She wanted the full tour. From top to bottom. Every nook. Every cranny.

But crannies—and nooks—could wait. Blue was too busy looking into Spencer's deep green eyes to worry about anything else. Smiling. Teasing. Shiver inducing. His attention was focused exclusively on her.

Blue would be a fool not to return the favor.

"Did you see my home run?"

Three hours later. After a celebration with his teammates. Dozens of interviews. Spencer still asked the question with the eagerness of a little boy. He played baseball with the passion of a kid.

The rest of the time? One hundred percent, full-grown man.

"I may have caught a glimpse."

"Won us the game."

"I know. You propelled your team into first place. Time to reserve my World Series tickets."

Blue teased. But the fans who had lived through every pitch. The ones who floated out of the stadium, bounced to their cars, only rehashed every moment of the game on the trip home.

She pitied anybody who tried to convince the loyal hordes that this wasn't the Cyclones' year.

"You're funny," Spencer said.

He had Blue trapped. Her back was to the poured concrete countertop. His hands braced on the surface, one on each side of her waist.

"You aren't the first man to tell me that today."

Inches from brushing his lips against hers, Spencer paused, his eyes narrowing.

"Anybody I should worry about?"

"I ran into Dale. I sort of told him about us."

Another time, Blue might have led Spencer on. Not to make him jealous. Light, playful fun. A game he'd recognize and eagerly join. But like the tour of his home, that would wait for another time.

When they were on firmer footing. *If* they made it past this *get to know each other again* phase.

Blue was tempted to look beyond the here and now. To imagine a future for them. But that would be getting ahead of herself. Ahead of *them*.

Baby steps.

The need to take things slow was a big reason why Blue drove herself to Spencer's house. He tried to talk her into riding with him. One car made more sense, he argued. She countered easily, reminding him that she had a job to get to in the morning.

Spencer pointed out that he could drive her home whenever she wanted. Blue reminded him that he needed his rest. She needed to be at work long before he did.

Blue didn't consider her excuse a lie. Everything Blue said was the truth. What she didn't add—what she was reluctant to share— was that—for the time being—the fewer people who knew about them, the better.

Right now, the list consisted of two names. Jordyn and Dale.

Keeping something so important from her best friend was out of the question. That Jordyn was Spencer's sister didn't matter. First and foremost, she was Blue's best friend. Sharing every aspect of their lives was second nature.

The fact that Jordyn was thrilled by the news didn't hurt. Especially in the face of how Dale reacted.

Her brother's less-than-enthusiastic response hadn't been a surprise. However, Dale had driven home Blue's belief that she and

Spencer would be better off keeping their relationship to themselves. Away from outside scrutiny.

"You told your brother about us? Okay."

From the expression on Spencer's face, Blue could tell he didn't see the problem.

"He wasn't thrilled."

Spencer sighed. "Hardly a surprise—all things considered. He'll get used to the idea. Given time."

"I asked Dale not to tell anybody."

"Ah." Spencer caught on quickly. And he didn't look pleased. "You want to keep us on the down low."

"For now," Blue rushed to explain. "Until—"

"Until you know if you can trust me."

Faced with a straight-to-the-point question, Blue couldn't lie. Not to Spencer.

Raising a hand to his cheek, Blue found the skin of his cheek smooth to her touch. A testament to the care he'd taken to shave away the afternoon—after game—stubble.

Blue smiled. Not a grand gesture in the big scheme of life. But so thoughtful. So considerate. So… Spencer.

A reminder. Without realizing, Blue had missed Spencer's small gestures. Things he did with her in mind. Things that never occurred to the other men she'd dated.

Without a big production that would draw attention to himself,

Spencer knew how to make Blue feel special.

When Blue asked herself why she let Spencer back into her life with so little resistance, the answer was simple. No matter how hard she searched, she never found a man who measured up to Spencer. She kidded herself into believing he no longer mattered. When in truth, he did.

Always had. Always would.

"I trust that you meant what you said. I believe you want to be with me. I know you want this to work."

"I hope you feel the same, Blue."

As Blue looked into Spencer's eyes, she willed him to believe her. Hoping he'd understand.

"The world moves so fast. When we first got together, we were in an insulated bubble. Even though you were famous, I don't remember feeling as though our every move was monitored. We could go out to dinner or to a movie. Take walks in the park without paparazzi jumping out from behind every other bush."

Blue paused, frowning.

"Am I wrong? Have I sugar coated the way things were?"

"No." Spencer shook his head. Closing his eyes, he rested his forehead against hers. "The world—*my* world—*has* changed in four years. Back then, I'd just crossed the line from up-and-comer to fully arrived. Now…"

"What you do—and who you're with—is news. Not just with

baseball fans. You've crossed over to celebrity status. Like it or not."

"Depends on the day." Kissing the end of Blue's nose, he moved to the refrigerator. He removed a bottle of wine, filling two glasses. He didn't ask if she wanted one. He didn't have to. "I won't lie. I enjoy the perks that go along with my status."

"I'll bet. The leggy model you were dating? Very nice perk."

"Janelle." Spencer handed Blue a glass "Not the brightest bulb. Kind of sweet. Uncomplicated."

Blue could have added interchangeable. The description certainly fit. Janelle was a beautiful woman. And for a man like Spencer. Rich, successful. A drop-dead sexy athlete. The model was one other thing. A cliché.

As if reading Blue's mind, Spencer's lips curved into a self-deprecating—yet unrepentant—smile.

"Can't blame me for fulfilling every man's fantasy."

"I don't blame you a bit," Blue said with absolute honesty. "Did you get them out of your system?"

"Beautiful women?" Spencer met Blue's gaze. His eyes, a warm, dark green, lingered over her every feature. "Apparently not."

Other men charmed. Now and then, Blue had found herself the object of such attention. She never took the flirting—or the men—seriously.

Spencer was a different breed. No matter his other faults—and there were plenty—when he spoke, he meant every word.

"I don't care about the paparazzi, Blue. Or internet trolls. I made my peace with all that crap long ago. However, I understand what you mean."

"Really?" Blue asked.

"Starting a new relationship is hard enough without millions of eyes watching. Our history will make the comments a bit more pointed. If staying under the radar is what you need, count me in."

"Not forever." Blue set her glass on the counter. In two short steps, she was in Spencer's arms. "Just until…" She shrugged.

"Just until," Spencer said firmly, putting the subject to rest. "You can stay the night?"

Smiling, Blue tugged at the collar of Spencer's shirt. The exposed skin, firm and wonderfully warm, felt like heaven against her lips.

"I packed my toothbrush. And a change of underwear."

As Blue continued her limited exploration, Spencer groaned with encouragement.

"Nothing else?" he asked, his fingers threading through Blue's hair, the clip that held the tresses in place falling to the floor.

"What did you have in mind?"

"Flannel. Nothing sexier than one of the long, voluminous Granny nighties. Drives me crazy."

Blue chuckled. Spencer's method of seduction was uniquely his own. Teasing and laughter. Followed by a long session of wild, steamy, mind-blowing sex. His method never failed. Not with her.

For her peace of mind, Blue decided not to contemplate his success rate with other women.

"Flannel. Check. I'll go shopping first chance I get."

"On second thought, never mind. I like you better without."

Blue let out a surprised gasp when Spencer lifted her into his arms.

"Without what," she asked.

"Clothing."

"Is that what we're doing? Getting naked?"

Blue had no objection. But she wanted to hear Spencer say the words. The sound of his voice—all deep and rumbly—made her blood heat.

"For starters. Four years is a long time. Getting to know your body again will take some time."

"Sounds like a plan." Teasing Spencer's ear with her lips, Blue whispered. "One that goes both ways."

"Jesus, Blue." Spencer speared her with his gaze. "I've missed you."

The kiss felt like a lifetime in coming.

Blue wrapped her arms around Spencer's neck, her fingers pressing into his scalp. How had she managed all these years without this—without his touch? Without his lips—so strong, so sure—against her?

A surge of desperation flowed through her. Blue needed more. The feelings were intense, clawing at her. Urging her to find a way—anything—to get closer.

As Blue's mind fogged over, her body writhed.

"Easy," Spencer rasped, his breathing harsh. "I don't want to drop you."

Blue groaned. *What was she thinking?* Instead of thinking with her libido, she should be worried that her antics might injure the Cyclones' star player.

"Put me down."

Spencer laughed. A little rough around the edges, but the sound was unmistakable.

"I was joking. I won't let you fall. I promise."

Blue pushed at Spencer's shoulder. A futile effort. His body was a long length of hard steel hewed by years of hard, concentrated effort. She considered herself to be in above-average shape. Her muscles were strong and well-toned. But against Spencer?

A baby bird's downy feather would have more luck toppling the Eiffel Tower.

"Never mind me." Frustrated, Blue let out a gust of air. "The Cyclones need you healthy. I can see the headlines now. *Kraig out*

MARY J. WILLIAMS

for the season with sex-related injury. Fans vilify girlfriend."

"I bet I went out happy."

"This isn't a joke." Blue appreciated Spencer's ability to find humor in almost everything. But not this time. "Freak accidents happen all the time. Even something as small as a pulled muscle could bench you for a week. Maybe more."

"What's your solution? No sex?"

"Okay." Blue didn't like the idea, but if the good of the team were at stake, she'd make the sacrifice. "Put me down. No sex."

Spencer let out a bark of laughter. From the look on his face, he expected Blue to join in. When she didn't, his expression changed from amused to exasperated.

"Are you worried about me, the team, or your job?"

Well, crap. Blue hadn't considered her job. Another reason not to continue. A few kisses from Spencer and her ambitions went up in a puff of rampaging desire.

"Yes, yes, and hell, yes," Blue answered Spencer's query in order. "Why aren't you concerned?"

Shaking his head, Spencer kept his arms firmly around Blue, ignoring her order to put her down. Purposefully, he started up the stairs.

"I know a guy who tweaked his back taking off his shirt. Couldn't swing a bat or field a ball. Missed ten games."

"What is the point of that horror story?"

"Simple. Shit happens, Bluebell. What am I supposed to do? Wrap myself in cotton when I'm not on the field?"

"Breathing might be a problem," Blue said thoughtfully.

When Blue caught Spencer's raised eyebrows, her eyes widened. Then, she grinned. What was wrong with her? Baseball had always been important. But the fact that she'd actually considered Spencer's ridiculous suggestion—however fleetingly—bordered on crazed fan territory.

Luckily, Blue had Spencer to pull her back from the brink.

"Oops."

"Oops, indeed." Once in his bedroom, Spencer set Blue on her feet. "If I wanted to live a celibate life, I'd have joined a monastery, not a baseball team."

"One in the Himalayas? With scratchy brown robes and a round bald patch shaved into your hair?"

"I weighed my choices carefully. The decision was a tough one. A warm, fan-filled stadium or a cold, mostly deserted monastery?"

As Spencer continued their conversation, he removed Blue's clothing, starting with the buttons on her jacket. One. Two. Three. Methodical. Slow. Yet somehow sexy as all get out.

"The brotherhood of baseball? Or the brotherhood—period."

Blue let her jacket slide down her arms. Getting into the spirit, she added, "Money, fame, beautiful women? Or none of the above?"

"Mm." Spencer trailed his finger along the line of Blue's jaw, his touch gentle. "There are a lot of things I could give up—if I had to. This isn't one of them."

"Sex?"

"You."

"Good answer."

"The *best* answer. Funny thing. The truth usually is."

Done with talking, Spencer slid his hand around Blue's neck. His eyes, so intensely green, held hers as long as possible before he claimed her mouth in a searching kiss that reached toward her heart.

"So many clothes. Why?"

Spencer made quick work of Blue's linen pants. The silk panties and matching bra followed, hitting the floor in an artless heap.

"The Cyclones frown at their employees showing up for work naked."

As he stepped back to survey his handiwork, Spencer nodded.

"I never minded sharing. Until now." Tanned from hours spent on a hot, sunny ballfield, Spencer's skin appeared even darker as his hand closed over Blue's pale, creamy breast.

"Mine."

One word. Simple yet telling. Blue would have argued. She

knew she should. Yet, how could she? He told the truth.

However, Blue wanted to make something clear. Belonging wasn't a one-way street.

Her grip firm, her gaze steady, Blue's hand covered his.

"Mine."

"Damn straight, Bluebell. Every inch." Spencer gave her a slow, enticing smile. "Now, what are you going to do with me?"

Blue didn't need the question twice. She'd imagined this moment a hundred times. A thousand. The scenario changed— depending on her mood. But the beginning never altered.

"Lose the clothes."

"There's nothing sexier than a woman who knows what she wants," Spencer said, stripping down without hesitation.

"Or a man who's willing to give it to her."

Another time, Blue would request a striptease. Emphasis on the tease. Tonight, she didn't have the patience. With a shove, she had Spencer on his back, her legs on either side of his lean waist.

"You're bigger than I remember."

"Really?"

Blue laughed when Spencer shifted his hips, his erection brushing the inside of her thigh.

"Not down there."

Spencer had been genetically blessed. Gorgeous face. Strong, naturally lean body. As for his penis? Long. Straight. Wonderfully hard when the occasion arose—so to speak. But best of all. He played his instrument like a virtuoso.

"I meant you're bigger up here." Blue touched Spencer's shoulders, her hands running down his muscled arms. "You were always well-built. But now…"

What more could Blue do but sigh? And devour him with her gaze.

"You seem more delicate," Spencer said. His wandering fingers came to rest on Blue's hips. "Yet somehow curvier."

"I like the differences."

"Me, too."

Spencer rose, his arms curving around Blue. He caressed her back, the line of her spine, the slope of her butt. His lips found hers. She sank into the kiss, the desperation was gone, but not the intensity.

Taking Blue with him, Spencer rolled to his side. His touch, so thorough, sent sparks of pleasure across her skin. The feel of his mouth on her breasts had her crying out, her fingers digging into the sheets as her back arched off the mattress

We've been here before, Blue thought as a haze enveloped her brain. Familiar yet wonderfully new.

The differences were inevitable. Time. Experience.

Blue wasn't the same young woman. Spencer had changed, too.

The chemistry remained. Undeniable as always. But if Blue

had expected to know what was coming. To anticipate Spencer's moves. She was wrong.

Amazingly, earth-shatteringly, mind-blowingly, in the best way possible, wrong.

"Did you moan like that before?" Spencer asked, raising his lips from where they were enjoying Blue's taste. His fingers kept playing between her legs.

The relentless barrage on her body made breathing a chore. How was she supposed to keep track of her accompanying soundtrack?

"What moan?"

Spencer slid his fingers a little deeper.

"That one."

"No. Maybe." Blue licked her lips. The next noise out of her mouth bordered on operatic. "You've learned a few new tricks. If my moans sound different, blame yourself."

"You don't say?"

Spencer sounded pleased and a little too cocky for Blue's liking. He'd always known how to play her body. In four years, he'd traveled from expert to master craftsman. If he wanted to bask in his accomplishments, let him.

Not right now!

Blue nudged Spencer in the thigh with her knee, careful to keep clear of a certain vital, distended organ. Another time. When she was no longer in desperate need of it or the man attached.

The way Blue felt at the moment. She didn't know when that would be. Sixty? Maybe seventy years from now?

"Why are you talking?" Blue asked. Taking Spencer's face between her hands, she made certain she had his full attention. "More action, less conversation. Understand?"

"Loud and clear, Bluebell."

The intensity of Spencer's gaze belied his teasing tone. Green fire swirled in his eyes. A telling sign.

Spencer wanted Blue. As much as she wanted him.

As Spencer settled between Blue's eagerly accommodating legs, his lips met hers.

"Wait." God, the man fogged her brain past all reason. "Condom," Blue gasped.

"Already suited up and ready for action."

When?

A second later, as Spencer slowly joined their bodies, Blue hazily wondered why she cared. About anything. Anything except this.

Spencer. The rush of feelings. Higher. Higher. Further than she imagined possible. Nothing else mattered. Nothing else ever would.

"I can't hold on much longer," Spencer ground out the words, sweat beading his brow. "But I need you with me, Blue."

Blue wrapped herself around Spencer. Arms. Legs. Body. Pounding so hard, her heart almost leaped from her chest.

Pleasure exploded from her toes to the top of her head. Radiant light burst in behind her eyes, blinding her to everything else.

Spencer collapsed, his body briefly blanketing hers before moving just enough to keep from crushing her, never losing contact.

Her head resting on Spencer's shoulder, her hair tangled around his arm, anchoring him. Tight and secure. Blue floated on a cloud. Exhausted in the best possible way.

What tomorrow would bring, Blue couldn't say. Honestly, she didn't care. Not now. She could worry about the future when she didn't have Spencer's arms around her. Or the steady beat of his heart under her hand.

"All's good?" Spencer asked, brushing his lips against Blue's temple.

Blue shut off her brain, closed her eyes, and continued to float. With a sigh, she smiled.

"All's good."

CHAPTER FOURTEEN

A TEAM CAN'T win a championship in April. But they can lose one.

Spencer knew the truth of these words. As did his teammates. A great record to begin a baseball season was no guarantee of a great ending.

One month down. Five to go. Nobody except their fans was handing the Cyclones the World Series trophy just yet.

However, a fast start felt a hell of a lot better than a slow one. The vibe in the locker room of a winning team was so much better than in a losing one.

The success of April carried over into May. And June. By July, Seattle was in first place sporting the best record in baseball. As a team, they were running on all cylinders. Hitting. Fielding. The atmosphere in the dugout was loose and easy.

On the field and off, the chemistry was the best Spencer could remember.

Ten Cyclones were voted onto the annual All-Star Game roster. Spencer led in the voting with their rookie phenom, Drake Langston, right behind.

"I wish I was going with you guys."

Spencer slapped Travis on the back. The fans had punched his friend's ticket to the game, but a nagging injury would keep him in

Seattle.

The three men were enjoying an after-game drink at their favorite out-of-the-way watering hole. The bar was dark. The beer cold. And most of the time, their fellow patrons left them in peace.

"No point in aggravating that sore elbow. We need you in August and September. I kind of wish I could stay here with you. A few days off would be nice."

Though he'd never missed a game, getting voted onto the all-star team still meant a lot to Spencer. Some called the mid-summer classic obsolete. A popularity contest whose time had passed.

At one time, fans enjoyed watching the American League face off against their National League counterparts. Other than the World Series, the two leagues never mingled. That changed with the advent of interleague play. A whole generation couldn't remember the game any other way.

Sorry haters. They could grouse all they wanted. Like night games. Or the designated hitter. The All-Star Game wasn't going anywhere.

"Of course, you want a few days off," Nick said. "If I had a woman like yours to keep me company, I'd blow off this game in a heartbeat. Nobody is making you go."

"I owe the fans."

"Bullshit." Nick wasn't as sentimental about baseball as Spencer. He was grateful to everything the game had given him.

And he loved playing. But he didn't hold the history in awe. "The fans want us to win. What do they care if you blow off a trip to Tampa Bay?"

"You're going," Spencer pointed out.

"What else am I going to do? I'm a sad son of a bitch who has no reason to go home at night."

"Boo hoo." Travis made an exaggerated pouty face. "Your stable of women is bigger than any I know."

"True." Nick looked pleased with the thought. "But none of them has anything on Blue."

"Too right," Travis nodded. "She's a keeper."

"Can't argue."

"I knew something was wrong." Letting out a sigh, Nick turned to Travis. "Have you ever seen such a hang-dog expression? Our man is on the top of the world. He's in the middle of another MVP-caliber season. That pretty face of his is plastered on every other bus and billboard in the city."

"And," Travis jumped in. "A gorgeous, funny, smart, sexy woman has welcomed him back into her life. When, let's face it, she had every reason to kick his sorry ass to the curb."

"I get the point, assholes," Spencer muttered into his beer.

"Does he?" Nick asked Travis, ignoring Spencer. "A month ago, our friend was happy as a clam. Grinning like a fool for no apparent reason."

"Except we knew the reason," Travis interjected.

"We did. But now? Why has the finish dulled on our good buddy's shiny new penny? Why—"

"For Christ's sake," Spencer slapped his hand onto the table. "Give it a rest, Oprah."

"I think he meant to insult me. But I like Oprah."

"Me, too." Travis clinked his bottle against Nick's. "Smart women with their own money make me hot."

Rubbing his face, Spencer's head fell back, his eyes closed in exasperation.

"Did you practice this routine? Because it could use some work."

"Pure improv." Nick signaled the barmaid to bring another round.

"Well, you suck."

"Just Nick? I thought I delivered my part with a certain finesse."

"Hey. I resent the implication."

Tuning out Travis and Nick's easy banter, Spencer paid for the drinks. He ignored the barmaid and her bright, encouraging smile. A pretty blonde with nice curves and an impressive cleavage, six months ago, she might have gained the attention she sought.

B.B. Before Blue.

Spencer didn't notice when the invitation on their server's face slipped. Or morphed into a disappointed frown. He wasn't immune. Simply not interested.

Blue had all his attention. Outside of baseball, she was the center of his universe.

When the Cyclones were at home, Spencer and Blue spent every night together. She had her job. He had his. But the only thing he wanted to do during his down time, was have Blue as near as possible.

Without a doubt, Spencer knew Blue felt the same. Her smile. The way she walked into his arms without hesitation. Snuggling close.

And the sex. Spencer felt himself harden just at the thought. They couldn't keep their hands off each other. If they weren't touching, the look in Blue's eyes felt like a caress. A promise of things to come.

Everything was perfect. Except...

One thing. Minor. Yet, like a tiny sliver left unattended, the problem had worked under Spencer's skin. An annoyance to start. Slowly, it was growing into something he couldn't ignore.

Spencer wouldn't verbally acknowledge Travis and Nick's jabs. But they were right. He wasn't as happy as he should've been and the reason was simple. He wanted to go public with their relationship, Blue wasn't ready.

Was Spencer's request so unreasonable? He didn't want to take out an ad. Or write the announcement in the sky. No fanfare. Just a dinner. In a restaurant. Or coffee at their favorite café.

Hell, at this point, Spencer would settle for a walk in the park. Something—anything—that took them into the light.

Sue him. Spencer was sick and tired of the shadows.

Unfortunately, Blue wasn't.

The dilemma had Spencer stymied. More and more, he felt Blue's reluctance stemmed from the fact that she still didn't trust him. Not completely. He wondered if she ever would. Though she said she was all in, he couldn't be certain.

Reasonable or not, telling the world that they were together would symbolize that Blue believed in him. In them.

Spencer pushed. Blue resisted. He was scared as hell of issuing an ultimatum. What if she gave a flat-out no? He couldn't lose Blue. Not again.

"Whatever is eating at you, Yoda? Fix it. Soon. Before the problem spills over onto the field."

"That will never happen," Spencer assured Nick.

Unbreakable, irrefutable rule number one. Personal issues stayed at home. Or—in an emergency—in the locker room. Once between the chalk, nothing messed with Spencer Kraig's head.

Not even a certain beautiful, stubborn, redhead.

"You better be right."

Spencer met Travis' gaze. His friend seemed easy going. The

laconic way he draped his long body in a chair. The slight Southern drawl. The way his lids hooded his dark blue eyes. But when something mattered, Travis could be the hardest of hardasses.

Baseball? Winning? They mattered.

A sliver of doubt crept into Spencer's mind. And he didn't like the feeling. Damn Blue. Life was so much easier when he didn't care about anything more than baseball. Easier. And, though he hadn't realized until recently, a lot lonelier.

There had to be a solution. Baseball wasn't going anywhere. Neither was Blue. He had to find a way to blend the two.

Holding up his drink, Spencer looked at his friends. His teammates. His brothers.

"When have I ever let you down?"

"Never," Nick said without hesitation.

"Not once," Travis echoed the sentiment.

Damn straight, Spencer thought, the sliver of doubt dissolving as quickly as it appeared. He had their backs. And he had Blue.

Now. Always. And come hell or high water. Forever.

"TAKE LAST MONTH'S figures and compare them to the last few years at this time. I want a broader outlook before I present the findings at tomorrow's meeting."

"Will do." Blue's new assistant nodded, jotting down notes.

Peri Winslow guarded Blue's office like a well-coiffed guard dog. Unlike Ernie—the young man who occupied the desk when she first arrived—Peri was neither sweet nor befuddled. She was efficient, bordering on obsessive.

In other words, exactly what Blue needed.

Without needing extensive details, Peri only had to observe the lay of the land for a few days to understand Blue's situation. And dealt with Vance Sutter accordingly.

Always respectful, Peri's arrival had changed the office dynamic. She didn't allow Vance's assistant to bulldoze past without an appointment. Phone calls were carefully screened. Nothing business related reached Blue unless Peri vetted it first.

Since the arrival of Peri—at Riley Preston's recommendation—Blue could finally breathe freely during work hours. Not that things were perfect. As long as Vance Sutter was in charge, perfections weren't possible. There were still the daily meetings that fluctuated between passive/aggressive bullshit and mumbled hostility.

Blue had come to terms with the fact that Vance pretty much hated everything about her. Even her red hair seemed to piss him. Now and then, he'd stare at the top of her head for several seconds before letting out a sigh, his lip curling into a sneer.

Whatever his problem—and there were many of them—Blue never reacted. Or commented. The meeting would continue. And if she were lucky, she wouldn't have to deal with him for the rest of the day.

"Your schedule is pretty light this afternoon. If you want to take an extra-long lunch, that shouldn't be a problem."

Blue smiled at the older woman. Except for the steely set of her eyes, Peri looked like the stereotypical grandmother. If grandma dressed in designer suits and wore heels that were the envy of every woman in the building.

Nearing sixty, Peri wasn't energetic as much as steady. As she put it, she was in for the long haul. Unflagging stamina and a sharp, nimble mind. Blue didn't know how she'd ever survived without her.

"A few glasses of wine wouldn't hurt," Peri added.

"Am I that obvious?"

"I know man trouble when I see it."

Blue frowned. "I thought you were happily married."

"Almost forty years." Smiling, Peri automatically straightened Blue's desk. "Which makes me an expert at dealing with a man *and* the trouble he can't help bringing with him."

Peri didn't strike Blue as a woman who would put up with a lot of nonsense. Not unless the man was worth it.

"Bart must be a good man."

"He is." The light in Peri's eyes was unmistakable. "He's the love of my life. And a pain in my backside. The little dear."

Peri's closed the door behind her. The woman was observant. Blue had trouble, the man variety. For weeks, she tried to figure out what to do before Spencer lost what little patience he had left.

The last thing Blue wanted was a blow-up. How was she supposed to avoid the unavoidable?

Grabbing her purse, Blue took out her phone. Sitting in her office wasn't getting her anywhere. As usual, Peri was right. Time for lunch. Extra-long sounded good. A glass or two of wine. But most of all, she needed advice.

Luckily, Blue knew just the person for the job.

"I'M GLAD YOU called."

"I'm glad you could get away at such short notice."

Riley Preston handed her menu to the waiter, having placed her order. A steak sandwich—medium rare. French fries—extra crispy. And a glass of wine—red.

Blue admired a woman who knew what she wanted. And since every bit sounded good, she ordered the same.

"Thank God you aren't one of those, *I only want a salad*, women."

Blue shrugged. "I like a salad. With bacon and hardboiled eggs. And croutons. And black olives."

"In other words, a little lettuce and a lot everything else," Riley laughed. "Amen and pass the dressing."

Riley's laughter drew attention from a nearby table of men out for a business lunch. Whether they recognized her or not, they certainly liked what they saw. Not that Blue blamed them.

Dressed in light blue, Riley's belted silk dress showed off her slender figure. Emphasizing her curves. Her skin glowed with health and happiness. A woman who was comfortable in her own skin.

"Is there a secret to oozing confidence?" Blue was ready to take notes.

"A good question. Not so long ago, I wanted the answer."

Blue couldn't imagine Riley as anything but the most together person she'd ever met.

"Really?"

Hearing the skeptical tone in Blue's voice, Riley nodded.

"I grew up here never thinking I'd ever leave. But something happened. A broken heart, to be exact." Riley said it casually as if broken hearts happened every day. Which, of course, they did. "After that, I didn't want to stay."

"But you came back."

"I grew up. *And*, I had the Knights. A football team is a pretty big incentive."

"May I ask who broke your heart?" When Riley didn't answer, Blue wanted to give herself a swift kick. They were easing into friendship. Some text. A few e-mails. A couple of phone calls.

They weren't at the point where unsolicited personal questions were welcome. "Tell me to go to hell. I won't mind."

"Believe me, if your question bothered me I would. Without hesitation. I paused because it's been awhile since I've thought about that part of my past."

"You're smiling? About a broken heart?"

"Am I smiling?" Riley raised a hand to her mouth. "Well, what do you know? I suppose a happy ending has a way of smoothing away the bad memories."

"Happy?" Blue frowned. Then the light dawned. "You mean Sean?"

Nodding, Riley sighed. "Sean was clueless. When he stomped on my heart—and make no mistake, that is what he did—he had no idea how I felt."

"Now he's your husband."

"True. We found our way. But there were a lot of highs and lows in between." Riley gave Blue a long, thoughtful look. "Do you want to tell me about yours?"

"My?"

"Broken heart."

"No longer broken," Blue said.

"That's good. But something is bothering you. Same man?"

Leaning closer, Blue lowered her voice. "Spencer Kraig."

"There's something about a man in uniform." Riley picked up

her glass, taking an appreciative sip.

"Spencer didn't set out to break my heart."

"But...?"

"It's a long story."

Eyes sparkling with interest, Riley relaxed in her chair.

"I have all afternoon."

Blue began slowly. But once she found her rhythm—and Riley showed herself to be an interested, compassionate audience—her story poured out.

"I like Spencer. But he was an ass."

Blue couldn't argue. "You know Spencer?"

"The sports world is surprisingly small. We've met at several charity functions. Sean knows him better than I do." Taking another sip of wine, Riley sent Blue a thoughtful look. "If I understand your problem, Spencer wants to take your relationship public. You don't."

"In a nutshell."

"Because...?"

"Right now, we're pressure free. Once the world knows about us, that's bound to change."

Riley nodded. "The first wave of publicity will be a shock. But like anything, that dies down."

"I know."

"You don't think your relationship is strong enough to handle a few prying eyes?"

"I think it is. But," Blue took a deep breath, ready to admit for the first time something that terrified her. "I'm afraid to find out. I don't want to lose Spencer again."

"I understand. Even now. And Sean and I are about as solid as two people can get."

When Blue and Spencer were alone. Laughing. Making love. Or simply sitting watching television, she'd have sworn that nothing could separate them. Doubt only trickled in when Spencer was on the road, and she let her imagination take over.

Placing a hand on hers, Riley drew back Blue's attention. "If you want a guarantee, I'm afraid you're out of luck."

Blue already knew that. But talking to somebody who came at her and Spencer with fresh, unbiased eyes helped.

"How have you managed?" Riley shared some of Blue's experiences. Not asking for advice would've been foolish.

"I can only tell you what works for me. Every time we hit a rough patch. Either from external forces or one of our own making. I let myself vent. Then I take a step back and ask myself one question."

Eager, Blue waited.

"What would my life be like without Sean?"

"Unthinkable," Blue answered. For Riley. And for herself.

Riley nodded. "There's your answer. Feel better?"

"Yes? No? Maybe?"

Picking up a fry slathered in ketchup, Riley grinned. "That sounds about right."

"Enough about men!" Blue gave herself a mental shake. "Pre-season games are about to start. Ready to bring another Super Bowl title back to Seattle?"

The Knights won their third championship last February. The first since Riley started running the team. If they won again next year, that would be two in her brief tenure. Impressive for anybody. But for a young woman navigating a male-dominated world? Freaking spectacular.

"Personally? I hate this time of year."

Surprised, Blue paused, her sandwich halfway to her mouth.

"Really? Why?"

"Pre-season games are nothing but a way for the rich to become richer." Obviously, a subject she felt passionate about, she frowned into her wine. "We pack fans into the stadiums to watch meaningless battles. And why? Because they're willing to shell out their hard-earned money, and we're greedy. We risk the welfare of young men whose shelf life is short to start with."

"Injuries."

"Exactly. Do you know the average length of an NFL career? Three point three years. After all the work and sacrifice, most players never get that big payday. And when they do? Very little of the money is guaranteed. My grandfather purchased the Knights before I hit my teenage years. Since then, I've seen some pretty brutal ends to promising careers. Strong yet amazingly fragile."

"I read the league was considering expanding the number of pre-season games."

"Over my dead body."

"You really care about your players." One more reason for Blue to worship the ground on which Riley Preston and her killer designer shoes walked.

"Maybe because I married a wide receiver. Plus, the love and respect for the game my grandfather instilled in me." Impassioned, Riley met Blue's gaze. "Football is the most popular game in the United States."

"I'm aware," Blue said. Baseball ran a distant second. But that was fine. Just made them work harder.

"Did I sound like a braggart?"

"Only a little."

Riley smiled, but the self-deprecating quality made her all the more likable. "My point was that we owners are so concerned with adding money to our already bursting coffers, sometimes we forget that the players on our fields are human beings."

"Also, grown men who know what they're doing," Blue pointed out. "High risk can lead to high reward."

"Not to mention that a lot of professional athletes are arrogant, misogynistic creeps. Makes me wonder why we love sports."

"Good question."

"What's the answer?" Riley asked.

"Hell if I know."

CHAPTER FIFTEEN

"I'VE NEVER BEEN so glad to see the end of July in my life."

"Turn the calendar, turn our luck."

Passing, Nick slapped Trevon Marks, the Cyclones center fielder, on the back.

"Stop blaming the month and try catching a fucking fly ball."

"Did you see that sun? Brutal." Travon squinted as if he were still on the field dealing with a high sky. "Lucky it didn't blind me."

"You were wearing sunglasses, asshole," Burt Collier reminded him. Because he was Travon's best friend and fellow outfielder, he could get away with the insult. Most men would be swallowing their teeth about now.

"Whiney little girls," Travis shook the head that hung between his legs. He was battling a slight case of the flu—a fact that he didn't share with anybody but Spencer and Nick. "We had a God-awful road trip. Shit happens. Time to get over themselves and worry about facing the Yankees tomorrow night."

Spencer shoved his gear into his bag. God-awful didn't begin to describe the past twelve games. Two measly wins against ten losses. Added to the fact that Houston—their division rivals—were on a white-hot streak meant the Cyclones had fallen out of first place for the first time all season.

211

Every player dreaded a slump.

Questioning himself. Wondering if he'd lost whatever magic he once possessed. Hits were a thing of the past. Even his glove turned against him. Balls that used to find the pocket with ease sailed through his legs. Runners he could gun down blindfolded scored from second as his throw to the plate missed the target by a mile.

Spencer wasn't immune. Luckily, during his career, the few slumps he experienced were of the mini variety. One solid knock, a stellar defensive play, or a long home run would end the problem as quickly as it began.

Yes, Spencer knew how a slump felt. What was happening to the Cyclones didn't have that feel.

"We need to clear our heads," Nick said, tucking his buttoned shirt into his pants.

The team had a strictly enforced road dress code. When the Cyclones traveled, the players had to wear a tie and jacket. Jeans were out. A few of the guys went all out. Expensive tailored suits. Shoes with a high shine. Spencer, Nick, and Travis stayed lower key—sports coats and slacks—saving the big guns for the post season.

"Any suggestions?" Travis asked. His gray tweed jacket was one of ten he switched out during the year.

"Figure skaters."

Spencer groaned, sending Travis a disgruntled look. "Why did you ask him that?"

"Because I love *Bull Durham*," Travis said, referencing perhaps the greatest baseball movie ever made. *If* the viewer was after a laugh. For tears? *Field of Dreams*. Every time. "*And* I love figure skaters."

"You're out of luck. Our plane leaves in an hour."

"I think we could come up with a figure skater or two in Seattle." Closing his bag, Nick grabbed his jacket. "Of course, in *Bull Durham*, they skipped the skaters, flooding the field instead. We're cute, but I don't think we could pull that one off without a major fine."

"And my boot up your asses."

"Relax, Yoda. What happened to your sense of humor?"

"I lost it around our sixth loss in a row."

Nothing sobered his friends faster than a quick reminder of where their season was headed. If the Cyclones didn't pull out of their tailspin soon, all dreams of postseason glory would be shelved for another year.

"Most of the guys in this locker room know how to get to the other side of a slump," Travis reminded his friends. "We need to concentrate on bucking up the less experienced players. In particular, our rookie phenom."

Spencer nodded, worried eyes moving to where Drake

Langston sat removed from his teammates. Something was up with the kid. Had been for several weeks.

"He won't admit anything is wrong. I asked."

"Me, too," Nick sighed. "Bought him a drink. Tried to get him laid. Half a beer and I thought he would slide off his barstool."

"Do you know what Langston did when I offered to set him up with a sure thing? *Blushed*, for Christ's sake. Redder than a fire truck." Travis couldn't seem to fathom the idea. "Do you remember the last time you fucking blushed?"

"What's a blush?" Deadpan, Nick stared wide eyed from Travis to Spencer.

"So, the kid is inexperienced." Spencer exited the locker room, sending one more glance Drake Langston's way. From his expression, he looked as if he'd lost his last friend. "I don't care if he's a goddamned virgin. We need him back on his game."

THE CYCLONES EEKED out a win the next night. Clinging to a nail-biting one-nothing lead heading to the ninth, Carlos Petretti, the team's flame-throwing closer struck out the first two batters.

With the count in his favor, Petretti and his catcher inexplicably went away from the pitcher's strength. Instead of a steady diet of fastballs, he nibbled at the corners. As a result, he walked the next two men he faced.

Joining the pitching coach on the mound, Spencer could see the sweat rolling off Petretti's face. That wasn't so bad. What worried him was the flicker of panic he saw.

"Breathe, Carlos. You own Dietrich. Give him some heat and let's hit the showers."

Petretti nodded. But Spencer's gut told him this wouldn't be an easy out. One pitch. Two. Three. None even close to the strike zone. With his fastball nowhere to be found, Petretti reared back and threw one of the worst pitches Spencer could remember.

With a known curveball killer at the plate, Petretti lobbed one. Worse, the pitch stayed flat. Not a curve in sight.

Over the roar of the anxious crowd, the crack of the bat rang in Spencer's ears. But he was ready.

Diving to his left, he made a play that happened so fast, blink and one would've missed.

Luckily, *SportsCenter* led with Spencer's defensive gem, letting Cyclones fans revel, and the entire nation marvel at the best third baseman in the game.

BLUE CHECKED HER pulse. Yup. Still beating. Though she wondered how many more games like tonight's her heart could withstand.

Wiping his palms, Clark O'Hara hugged his wife, his oldest daughter, his youngest, his son-in-law. He gave his son a hearty slap on the back.

"Damn close. But I'll take it."

"The team needed this win," Dale said.

Now that the drama was over—and the good guys came away victorious—appetites returned. The food that sat untouched on the coffee table during the tense late innings disappeared.

"I'm glad you decided to watch the game with us instead of going to the stadium." From the kitchen, Connie O'Hara handed Blue a stack of napkins. "Put those next to the dip, sweetheart."

"Why *aren't* you at the game?" Dale asked, his voice too low for anybody else to hear. "Trouble in paradise?"

Blue had no intention of sharing the details of the problems between her and Spencer. Before the last road trip, they hadn't parted on the best of terms. Not exactly an argument. However, the tension was thick—and growing.

They spoke a few times. Briefly. Blue didn't want to get into anything heavy over the phone. Besides, she couldn't decide if the distance in Spencer's voice had to do with them, or the team's bad play.

Blue had gotten used to Spencer arriving at her door no matter how late the team plane arrived at SeaTac. Last night, he texted her, that was all. Four short words. *Back safely. Talk soon.* Hardly encouraging.

The night lasted forever. The day seemed even longer. Blue

waited for Spencer's call. She checked her phone a dozen times for a message. Anything to let her know that he wanted her at the game.

As the afternoon wore on, Blue debated making the first move. By the time she left for home, she'd convinced herself that not talking was for the best. Spencer needed to concentrate on baseball, not her. He'd call when the time was right.

"Spencer and I are fine," Blue assured Dale, shoving a napkin at him when guacamole slipped from his chip onto the front of his shirt.

"Just fine. Not great? Fantastic? Magical?"

"What are you? A thirteen-year-old girl? Honestly, Dale. What would you think if I used the word magical to describe my relationship?"

"That you were trying too hard."

"Exactly. I don't live in a YA romance novel. Thank God." Blue's phone buzzed. Spencer. "Excuse me."

As she slipped from the room, Blue answered without looking to see who was on the other end.

"Amazing ending," Jordyn said a little breathlessly.

Not Spencer, Blue's shoulder's slumped. She should've known. He had interviews, a shower, and a press conference to get through. Taking time to call his girlfriend wouldn't be high on his list of priorities.

"Spencer saved the game. I imagine your dad is floating."

"Mom might pry him off the ceiling in an hour or two. If she's lucky," Jordyn chuckled affectionately.

Picturing Byron Kraig, his chest puffed out with pride, Blue smiled.

"You stayed for the game?" Mondays were Jordyn's usual dinner with her family nights. "Normally you're only good for an inning or two."

"I've been traveling so much lately, spending some time with Mom and Dad felt like a good idea. As an added bonus, big brother decided to play hero. All around, a pretty good night at the Kraig house."

Hearing the pride in Jordyn's voice, Blue's smile widened. For all the times she groused about her family's—and best friend's—obsession with baseball, she reveled in Spencer's success right along with the rest of them.

"How are you doing? Have you and Spencer cleared the air?"

Blue leaned against the wall. The one covered with photos of her family through the years. Her eyes came to rest on her parents on their wedding day. Happy then. Happy now.

So many years. Ups and downs. Triumphs and heartaches. But no matter what came their way, Blue's parents faced the good and the bad together.

That's what Blue wanted. With Spencer.

"What is wrong with me?"

"Generally speaking?" Jordyn teased as only a best friend could. "Or do you want specifics?"

Blue felt an urgency. A need to find Spencer. Now. But as she rushed to the hall closet, pulled out her jacket, found her car keys in her pocket, she felt a lightness that had been missing for weeks.

"I need to go."

"Okay," Jordyn said, unaware of what was going on in Blue's head. "Lunch on Wednesday? I'll come by your office around noon."

"Fine. Great. Bye."

"Wait. You didn't answer my question. You and Spencer? What's the latest?"

"Ask me on Wednesday."

"But—"

Blue cut Jordyn off with a swipe of her thumb.

What to do, what to do? Rushing to the ballpark didn't make any sense, she decided. Maneuvering through the crazy downtown after-game traffic would be a nightmare. By the time she arrived, the only people left would be the clean-up crew.

Home was the smartest move. Spencer would look for her there. Or he would if she did her best to point him in that direction.

Shaking out her suddenly nervous fingers, Blue raised her phone, pulling up Spencer's number.

"Meet me at my place. Please. Please. Please. I need to see you tonight. I'll be waiting."

Taking a deep breath, Blue hit send. The rest was up to Spencer.

"Mom? Dad?" Blue called out. She found her family where she left them. Eating. Laughing. Rehashing the game. "I'm going to leave."

"Already?" Frowning, Clark looked at his watch. "It's later than I realized. Give your old man a hug. And drive safe."

"I will." Blue gave herself a moment to savor the comfort of her father's strong arms.

"Will we see you before Sunday dinner?" her mother asked, brushing her lips across Blue's cheek.

"Probably not." Blue took a deep breath. Now was as good a time as any. "Do you mind if I bring a friend?"

"Of course not. There's always room at our table," Connie assured her. "Anybody we know."

"Spencer."

Connie's eyes widened, obviously expecting any name but that one.

"Spencer Kraig?"

"Yes." With another quick hug, Blue waved, heading toward the front door. "We've been seeing each other for several months."

"Blue—"

"See you Sunday."

The buzz of voices followed Blue out of the house. She'd dropped a bombshell. Hopefully, the damage wasn't too extensive. Mostly surprise, she imagined. But whatever the mess, she'd have to deal with it later. Right now, she had something much more important to worry about.

Starting her car, she took the time to send one more text. Satisfied, butterflies taking wing in her stomach, Blue pulled from her parking spot and headed home.

And, fingers crossed, Spencer was headed there, too.

CHAPTER SIXTEEN

SPENCER GLANCED AROUND the mostly deserted locker room, remembering how loud and raucous things had been a short time ago.

A big believer that one game—one moment in that game—could turn the tide of an entire season, he nodded, putting a period on a damn good night.

Had this been that game? Ask him again at the end of the season. But Spencer felt in his bones that something had shifted. An attitude adjustment, so to speak. Tomorrow, his team would reassemble and play another one. Then another. And another.

We can only play them one at a time. The old adage fit baseball better than any sport. But that didn't mean certain games didn't have more impact than others. From the smiles plastered on the players' faces, Spencer believed this—the first of August—was one of those nights.

Taking a moment, Spencer scrolled through the messages on his phone. Nothing that couldn't wait until morning. Until he found Blue's text.

"Meet me at my place. Please. Please. Please. I need to see you tonight. I'll be waiting."

Spencer wanted to see her. More than he could say. He missed Blue. So much he decided to put their differences aside. At least for one night. If he didn't kiss her—and soon—he'd go crazy.

Then he heard a beep. Another text from Blue.

"FYI? I told my parents about us. Step number one. Number two? Dinner. You and me. In public. Any night. The restaurant of your choice."

"Damn, Bluebell. You're full of surprises," Spencer whispered, grinning.

"Yoda?"

Spencer jumped a foot. Swinging around, he found Drake Langston standing behind him.

Laughing at himself, Spencer patted his chest. "Watch it, kid. My heart isn't as young as it used to be."

Drake looked at the ground. At his shoes. At the wall. Stooping, Spencer tried to catch the rookie's skittish gaze.

"What's up?"

"Can I talk to you?"

Finally. Whatever was eating at the kid, he'd kept the details close to his vest. Spencer tried multiple times to get Drake to open up but to no avail.

Spencer didn't push. He respected a man's right to privacy. But he made certain Drake knew he had a friend if he ever needed a sympathetic ear.

Spencer slung an arm around Drake's shoulders.

Blue waited. But if anybody would understand the reason for

his delay, she would.

"My time is yours."

"Some place private."

Spencer steered Drake toward the manager's office. Nobody would disturb them there.

"Take a seat."

Drake wiped his hands on his dark pants. He didn't look old enough to shave. Spencer couldn't imagine what kind of trouble could plague such a clean-cut, clean-living young man. But at the moment, he looked as if he carried the weight of the world on his shoulders.

"Nothing can be that bad."

"Yes, it can."

"Okay." Spencer took a seat facing Drake. "Why don't you start from the beginning?"

"The beginning? Of this mess?" Taking a deep breath, Drake nodded. "Two years ago. My senior year in college..."

BLUE KEPT TELLING herself to go to bed.

Checking her phone every five seconds was neither productive nor wise. The smart thing—for the sake of her mental health— would be to brush her teeth, remove her makeup, and get some sleep.

The hell with Spencer. If he weren't man enough to at least

send her a *screw you* text, then she wouldn't waste another moment worrying. Or pacing. Or tearing her hair out.

Blue accomplished two of her goals. Clean teeth and a freshly scrubbed face stared back from the mirror over her bathroom sink. But she knew that sleep was out of the question.

Instead of tossing and turning in her big, cold bed, Blue opted for a cup of tea and an old movie. As if TCM read her mind, the station was running one of her favorites.

The Awful Truth. Crackling with wit and laugh-out-loud humor, the screwball comedy was the perfect way to take her mind off her problems. Or so she hoped.

As she settled down in front of the television, snuggled in her favorite blanket, her phone charging in another room, Blue tried to concentrate on the antics on the screen. Unfortunately, not even Cary Grant and Irene Dunne had the power to keep Spencer from invading her thoughts.

The feminist in Blue balked at what she could only identify as classic needy behavior. *You can live without a man for a few hours*, she reminded herself. *Or days. Even weeks and months. Get over yourself. Spencer is probably exhausted from the game. He'll call. And if he doesn't, so what?*

The other side of Blue's brain, the less evolved part, wasn't buying the logical side's hard sell.

You had your second chance. Something most people never get.

Spencer did his part. He proved to you that he wanted your relationship to work. But were you willing to meet him halfway? Nope. Your way, or the highway. Well, congratulations. You can enjoy your victory. Alone. Forever.

Damn. Her less-evolved side was a bitch.

Blue wrapped her hands around her cup. The warmth seeped into her hands as she sipped the hot, herbal tea. Ugh. Why had she chosen herbal tea? Because when she reached into her cupboard for the ubiquitous Earl Grey, she heard Jordyn reminding her that caffeine was a bad idea this late at night.

Another voice in her head. Just what Blue *didn't* need.

Caffeine wasn't her enemy—no matter what Jordyn claimed. Blue wanted tea. The real stuff. Dark. Bracing. She wasn't going to sleep; shouldn't she have something to help her get through the long hours ahead?

Grabbing her cup, Blue pushed her blanket aside and headed for the kitchen. She dumped the offending contents into the sink. Just as she reached for the canister of loose leaf tea that sat near her electric kettle, the doorbell rang.

Spencer. He was the only person allowed up without announcing him first.

Blue glanced at the clock. 1:17 a.m. Her first instinct was to zip across the room and pull him through the door. No questions asked. Or, she could ignore him. Let him stew the way she had the last few hours.

Settling on something in between, Blue chose to stroll—not rush. Her heart raced, why should she?

Calm and casual, Blue decided as she turned the knob. She was determined. Until she looked into Spencer's eyes. Those intensely green, irresistible, made her melt with a single glance, eyes.

Blue jumped without hesitation. Because she knew Spencer would catch her. And because she couldn't wait one more second to be in his arms.

"It's about time," Blue said before fusing her lips to his.

Spencer didn't disappoint. Anchoring her to him with one strong arm, his hand cupped the back of Blue's neck, massaging the tender skin. The thoroughness of his kiss a testament to how long it had been since his last taste.

"Hello to you, too," Spencer said, finally coming up for air.

"I've missed you," Blue whispered, her mouth brushing his ear. "Come inside, and I'll show you how much."

"That will have to wait."

Blue was too interested in the feel of Spencer's soft hair against her cheek to care, but she asked anyway—just to be polite.

"Why?"

"We have company."

Frowning, Blue raised her head, catching sight of another person standing to Spencer's left.

Drake Langston.

"Hello, Ms. O'Hara. Sorry about this. Maybe I should go."

"Don't be ridiculous. Please. Come in." Blue pushed at Spencer's shoulder. Carefully, with a last sweet kiss, he set her on her feet.

"You could've said something sooner," she hissed.

"I was a little preoccupied with your tongue down my throat." To his credit, Spencer lowered his voice so Drake couldn't hear.

As she straightened her robe, Blue checked her image in the hall mirror. Hardly company ready. Her hair was a mess, the clip that had held it in place hung precariously to one side. At least that was an easy fix. With the ease provided by years of practice, she wound the red strands into a simple topknot.

"Sit," Blue told Drake. He complied, his backside barely hugging the edge of the sofa cushion.

Blue didn't know the young man very well, but he'd never struck her as the nervous type. Tonight, he looked like he was about to jump out of his skin. Whatever was going on, he had the look of someone who wished he was anyplace but here.

"I was about to make myself a cup of tea. Spencer?" Blue jerked her head toward the kitchen. "Want to help?"

"Sure. Be right there." Spencer gave Drake a comforting pat on the arm. "Try to relax. And breathe. You won't do yourself any good if you fall over and give yourself a concussion."

"Well," Blue asked, handing Spencer the kettle to refill. "What's going on?"

"First. Thank you for acting as if this kind of thing happens every day?"

"Maybe this is normal. Enjoying late-night visits from gorgeous ball players? Doesn't that sound like me?"

As Blue lifted the lid of the baseball-shaped cookie jar, filling a plate with her mother's chocolate chip cookies, Spencer lightly bumped Blue's hip with his. A smile lit his face.

"No, Bluebell. Unless you mean me, that doesn't sound like you at all."

"Mm. I suppose not. Never mind. Tell me why I'm playing hostess to Drake Langston." Blue's eyes widened as she connected the dots. She worked in PR. Which sometimes meant damage control. "Please tell me he didn't hit somebody with his car. While driving under the influence."

"Nothing like that. But—"

"Should I call a lawyer?" Blue's brain clicked into professional mode. "The Cyclones have an excellent firm on retainer."

"Slow down." Spencer took Blue by the shoulders, his eyes meeting hers. "Drake hasn't done anything criminal. He hasn't committed a felony or a misdemeanor. I doubt the kid jaywalks. A lawyer might be necessary. Eventually."

"Why—?"

"Let Drake tell you his story. Just listen? I promised him you would know what to do. Sorry if I overstepped. This is a sensitive matter, and you're the only person I trust not to fuck it up."

Blue felt a wave of pleasure sweep through her. She was good at her job. And while she didn't *need* Spencer's affirmation, knowing he believed in her was like a shot of warm honey through her veins. Better than any drug. And she suspected, highly addictive.

Arranging mugs, plate, and a few napkins on a tray, Blue left Spencer to the heavy lifting. Once everything was in the living room, she handed Drake his tea. Something told her that he didn't need coddling. Rather than putting herself next to him, she took the opposite chair, crossed her legs, and waited.

"The floor is yours, Drake," Spencer said, sitting on the sofa.

Drake swallowed. His eyes were focused in Blue's direction, but not at her. At the vase she inherited from her grandmother.

"Somebody is blackmailing me."

Blue didn't react, her face keeping a neutral expression. In spite of her casual attire, she was all business.

"Somebody? Does that mean you don't know who the blackmailer is?"

"I know." Heat entered Drake's eyes. A little anger could be a good thing. Better than misery. "A man I thought was my friend. Andy Franklin. He…" Drake swallowed hard. "We were lovers."

Blue let the information sink in. Drake was gay. Hardly shocking. And no big deal. Except for the fact that he played baseball. With a few minor exceptions, the integration of homosexuality into professional sports was non-existent.

After years of hypocrisy, the military had finally abolished *don't ask, don't tell*. But where baseball, football, basketball, etc., were concerned, the arcane rule was alive and—for want of a better word—well.

Unofficially, of course. Owners would never say such a thing in public. But they were happy with the status quo. Gay men were welcome. As long as they kept their sexuality out of the locker room and behind *very* closeted doors.

"Your ex-lover? You haven't spoken since college?"

Blue's matter-of-fact reaction seemed to help Drake relax. For the first time, his shoulders lost a bit of their stiffness. He settled farther back on the sofa, taking his first sip of tea.

"About a month before I graduated, we broke up. Or, I broke up with him. Coming out wasn't an option. And truthfully? Even if declaring myself as a gay man had been possible, I wasn't ready for a serious relationship. Andy said he understood."

"You parted on good terms?"

"I thought so." Drake looked genuinely perplexed. "Andy even gave me a party the day before I left for my first minor league camp. We hadn't been together for months but still talked occasionally. The party was a really nice surprise."

Skip ahead two years. On the cusp of becoming a superstar, Drake was a sitting duck for an unscrupulous bastard with no qualms over leveraging an old relationship to cash in.

"When did Andy contact you and what did he say? Exactly."

"Six weeks ago. Just after the All-Star team was announced."

"The first time you were named to the squad."

Spencer and Blue exchanged looks. The disgust she saw in his eyes mirrored what she felt.

"Andy congratulated me. And I was happy to hear from an old friend. Keeping in touch with people I used to know isn't easy. And there are only a few who know about my..."

Blue hated watching Drake struggle to say the words. But she couldn't help. Unable to live—love—in the open? The thought was beyond her imagination.

"Did he ask for money right away?"

"No. We spoke a few more time over the next week. Catching up. Reminiscing. Softening me up so I wouldn't see the big blow coming," Drake said bitterly.

Blue wished she had the words to wipe the anguish from the young man's eyes. But she didn't. All she could do was help him get past this betrayal with as little fallout as possible.

"How much does he want?"

"Fifty thousand."

"To start," Spencer added. "This guy is savvy enough to understand Drake's rookie contract isn't a lot. The price is bound to increase along with the kid's salary."

"Until?" Blue asked.

"Hell if I know. The day I die?" Closing his eyes, Drake's head fell forward. "Andy left his demands open ended."

"But the threat was clear." Angry, Spencer paced. "If Drake doesn't pay, somebody is going to."

The story was juicy. And worth quite a bit to somebody with enough details.

"Does Andy have any proof that you were lovers? Pictures? Letters? An email or a text?"

Drake shook his head. "But does proof really matter?"

Only in a court of law. The court of public opinion was harder to predict. Drake could be skinned alive and left to flap in the wind. Or, because he wasn't a household name, the story might come and go, only a blip on the social media radar.

Blue set her cup on the table next to the untouched cookies. Time to get down to brass tacks.

"Do you want to come out?"

"No," he said firmly.

But Blue could see the want that flashed in Drake's eyes. If he hadn't been given the gift of an athlete's body and the discipline needed to turn himself into a world-class baseball player, he'd probably live his life as a proud gay man.

Blue hated the fact that sports still bred the myth that a gay man couldn't compete on the same level as what the homophobic culture considered a *real* man.

"Do you want to pay what could turn out to be a lifetime's worth of hush money?"

"Hell no," Drake was emphatic. "But…"

"Let me rephrase the question. If you pay the money, what guarantee do you have that Andy won't break his silence? Next year? Or the year after?"

"Do you want to live with that threat over your head?" Spencer asked.

"I don't know," Drake shouted, dropping his head into his hands. "I don't know."

For the first time since they started, Blue let her demeanor soften. She moved to the sofa, placing her hand on Drake's back.

"Give yourself some time to think about your options."

"I don't have time."

Frowning, Blue looked at Spencer.

"Andy Franklin gave a deadline. If the money isn't paid by game time tomorrow, he'll spill the dirty truth to the media." Spencer frowned. "Franklin's words, not mine."

If Drake were her brother, she'd slap him upside the head. Why had he waited until the last minute to go to Spencer? Why hadn't he given them more time to figure out a strategy?

As soon as she asked herself the questions, Blue knew the answers. Because after living for so long in fear, Drake was afraid of coming out on his own.

"Part of me hoped Andy would change his mind." Drake's laugh didn't have a hint of humor. "I haven't been able to sleep. Or eat. What will I do without baseball?" Panic entered Drake's eyes. "I don't have anything else."

Now wasn't the time to point out how wrong Drake was. He was a young man. There were always options. But he wouldn't believe her. To be honest? If she were in his shoes? Neither would she.

Drake felt as if his world was crashing down around him. Blue's job was to make certain that didn't happen.

"There's nothing we can do tonight. Go home. Try to get some rest. And think about what you want."

"I want to play baseball."

"As an outed gay man? Because if everything you've told me is accurate, that will be your only option."

"Is coming out and playing ball even possible?"

The hope in Drake's eyes felt like a stone in Blue's stomach. She wanted to assure him. *Yes. Of course. Stop worrying. Everything will be fine.* She couldn't say the words because she didn't know if they were true. She wouldn't give Drake false hope.

But, Blue could give him enough hope to get him to tomorrow.

"Here's what I know. Strictly fact. No bullshit."

"Listen up, rookie. Blue is the master of the no-bullshit straight talk."

Blue smiled at Spencer. His confidence—his belief that she'd do her best to make things right—was the shot of courage she needed.

"You have three big assets on your side. First? This isn't twenty years ago. Or ten. Or even five. Despite the prejudice that still exists—something you know a lot more about than I do—we live in a much more open-minded era. Not perfect by any means. But better.

"Second? A talent like yours doesn't come along every day. Once in a generation. Isn't that what you told me, Spencer?"

"Maybe." Spencer shrugged. But his lips twitched, turning into a smile that told a different story. "Don't let a little praise go to your head. If I see that head of yours start to swell, I won't hesitate to pull you back down to Earth. Understood?"

The threat seemed to lift Drake's spirits, Blue noticed. Spencer knew the truth, yet still treated him like one of the boys. The spark of hope Blue had been looking for.

"My point is this. The Cyclones need you more than you need them. If they were to cut you, or arrange a trade, the backlash against the team would be crippling. But I don't think you have to worry about losing your job. Ross Burton is no fool."

"What about my teammates? How will they react?"

"There will be players who don't want to share a locker room with a gay man. Though chances are pretty good that at some point in their careers, they already have."

"Probably in high school."

For the first time, Drake's laugh sounded genuine, not forced. Music to Blue's ears.

"No doubt. You'll have to deal with the backlash. But you have a big advantage. Asset number three. Spencer Kraig has your back." Blue met Spencer's gaze. "I don't know if you're facing a battle from some of your teammates, but if you are? I can't think of anybody I'd rather have on my side."

A current of charged electricity flowed between Blue and Spencer. Though he stood across the room, she felt his touch. Blue's breath caught in her chest. Like a caress. Warm. Comforting. And, oh, God, *loving*.

Blue blinked back the need to cry. Not the time or the place. Those words had practically become their motto. But there was no way in hell she'd embroider them on a pillow.

Their time had come. Blue and Spencer. Never mind the pillow. She wanted to carve their names in stone.

But Drake had to come first. Blue walked him to the door.

"I'll call you in the morning. First thing. If you still want to go ahead, I'll take care of everything with management. But if you change your mind—"

"I won't," Drake said firmly.

Blue believed him. But she wanted to give him an out. Just in case.

"We'll talk. You're taking back your power, Drake. I won't make a move unless you're one hundred percent on board."

"Thank you." Drake moved to hug Blue, reconsidering at the last second.

"You can't get away that easily," Blue said, taking him in her arms. He held on tight. A little too tight, but Blue didn't object. She hugged him back, giving him all the time he needed. When he finally pulled away, he blinked, clearing away the moisture from his eyes.

"I can get home on my own," Drake assured Spencer.

"You're stuck with me, kid." Spencer punched Drake on the arm. A cliché, but one that fit the moment perfectly. "Give me a second? I'll meet you at the elevator."

Smiling, Drake gave Blue and Spencer some privacy.

"Not exactly how I pictured this evening playing out."

Blue walked into Spencer's arms, resting her head on his chest. With a sigh, she nodded.

"I didn't see that curve ball coming."

Brushing his lips across Blue's forehead, placing a finger under her chin, he tipped her head. His eyes. Such a beautifully intense green. She could look at them—at him—forever without ever losing the feeling of wonder.

"You ran down Drake's assets. Most eloquently, by the way. But you forgot the most important one."

"What's that?"

"You."

Spencer's kiss was ever so soft, but the impact reached all the way to Blue's heart.

CHAPTER SEVENTEEN

AFTER SPENCER AND Drake left, Blue hadn't bothered to go to bed. Instead, she sat at her desk and carefully formatted a strategy. The end result was simple and to the point, magnifying the pros of the situation. Ross Burton and his board of directors could worry about the cons.

After a quick shower, Blue fashioned her hair into a low ponytail, a long line of glistening red down the center of her back. She took extra time with her makeup, covering the slight circles under her sleep-deprived eyes.

Understanding that concealer could do only so much. Blue had a lot to say this morning. Why not frame her words with a bold coral color that said, look at me.

Dressing for battle—her version—Blue picked her outfit carefully. She didn't know what to expect when she entered Ross Burton's office. But she wanted to look like a professional.

Still, Blue was a woman in a man's world. Why try to hide the fact? The light-yellow, fitted skirt and cream-colored silk blouse suited her mood perfectly. A dark-yellow belt and patent-leather pumps were perfect accents. And the four-inch heels gave Blue a nice boost. To her height and confidence.

Fastening a pair of antique silver earrings, Blue decided she was ready. Until her eyes caught sight of an item on the bookshelves near the closet door. She hadn't opened the box in years. Hadn't wanted to.

Every time Blue considered tossing the box, a kind of perverse sentimentality would overwhelm her. She used to curse weakness. Now, she was grateful for it.

Opening the lid, she reached in, unfurling a platinum chain. Hanging from a small loop was a bluebell made of sapphires.

Blue fastened Spencer's gift around her neck. She hadn't realized how much she'd missed the feel of it against her skin.

A smile on her face, Blue checked her satchel, making certain she hadn't forgotten anything. In the elevator, she took out her phone. Spencer answered on the first ring.

"Morning, gorgeous."

"Morning, handsome."

Spencer chuckled. "For a couple of people who didn't get any sleep, we sound damn chipper."

"How do you know I didn't sleep?"

"Because, I know you, Bluebell."

Blue's hand went to her neck, the sapphires warm to her touch.

"Where are you?" Blue asked when she heard the sound of laughter in the background and music. Bruno Mars if she wasn't mistaken.

"My place," Spencer said.

"Are you having a party? And why wasn't I invited?"

"Travis and Nick dropped by for breakfast. You know Nick. He can't be in a room for longer than thirty seconds without blasting his tunes."

"Nick and Travis just happened to drop by?" Blue asked, stashing her satchel in the backseat of her car.

"I may have called them. As soon as I explained the situation, I couldn't have kept them away. Travis never turns down the chance to make his famous pancakes."

Blue slid behind the steering wheel. Spencer had some pretty special friends. Drake needed their support and bam, there they were. The next time she saw Travis and Nick she would give them both a big, sloppy thank you kiss.

"Before you ask. Drake hasn't wavered. If anything, he's more determined than ever to stop his blackmailing ex in his scumbag tracks."

"How he's holding up?" Blue, switching to her in-dash phone as she put the car in drive.

"Stronger than he thinks. He'll be fine."

"I have an appointment with Ross Burton at nine o'clock."

"How did you manage that on such short notice?" Spencer sounded impressed.

"For all his easy-going charm, Ross is a businessman who keeps a close eye on his investments. I told his assistant that I had vital information that could seriously affect the Cyclones. Time-sensitive information. He cleared his calendar."

"So damn smart."

"Yes," Blue agreed, seeing no reason to dissemble. When the man was right, he was right. "Drake should be there, Spencer. Or at the very least, he needs to send a representative who will have his best interests at heart. Whatever is decided in Ross' office, he should have a say. A big, vocal one."

"Okay. I'll talk to Drake."

"Good."

Blue breathed easier. She'd do her best to take care of Drake. No matter her personal feeling, in the end, she was management. Low level with little power. Drake had all the leverage, and he needed to use it.

"Take care, Blue."

Hanging up, Blue spent the rest of the familiar drive to the Cyclones' headquarters mentally finetuning her presentation. She arrived an hour early. Exactly as planned.

"Good morning, Ms. O'Hara." Peri looked up from her computer in surprise. Try as she might, Blue couldn't persuade her assistant to drop the formality. Not wanting to alienate the woman, she didn't push the issue.

"I have a meeting with Mr. Burton's in an hour. Do you know if he's arrived yet?"

"I can find out. If not, would you like me to let you know when he gets here?"

"Please. And coffee, Peri. Black. In the biggest cup you can find."

"Right away."

Blue never drank coffee. But this morning, she'd make an exception.

"Anything else? Have you eaten breakfast?"

"I don't think my stomach could take anything solid."

For all her assistant knew, Blue could be suffering the after-effects of a wild night out. Peri, ever efficient and discreet, didn't ask for details.

"Oh. One more thing. Make a note to inform Mr. Sutter about the meeting."

"Really?" Peri asked, her pencil poised above her ever-present notebook.

"Fifteen minutes *after* the start."

Nodding, Peri scribbled the information, a small smile curving her lips.

"I DIDN'T EXPECT to see you this soon. But I shouldn't be surprised."

"Drake asked. I said yes." Spencer looked Blue up and down. "Don't you look like a breath of fresh air?"

"I was going for professional yet feminine."

"Mission accomplished."

Blue arrived at Ross Burton's reception area fifteen minutes early. Partly because she hated to be late. Mostly, because she couldn't stand another moment pacing the small confines of her office.

She and Spencer arrived simultaneously.

"And don't you look spiffy."

Spencer posed for her as if on the cover of a magazine—not an unfamiliar location for his photo-friendly face and body. The light gray single-breasted jacket and perfectly creased pants fit as if made for him. Which they were. Hair perfect. Face freshly shaven. Spencer looked more like a well-heeled businessman than a rough-and-tumble athlete.

Either way, Blue found him irresistible.

He straightened his already immaculate tie.

"Blue is my favorite color."

When this was over, and they were finally alone, Blue planned on messing up his perfect suit and tie. In ways they both would thoroughly enjoy.

"Mr. Burton will see you now, Ms. O'Hara."

"Here we go."

"Blue." Ross Burton rose from behind his desk. "And Spencer. What a nice surprise."

"Hold that thought," Spencer said, shaking Ross' hand.

245

Eyes narrowing, the jovial host turned into the cautious team owner.

"Would you like to explain?"

Ross directed the question to Blue. He indicated for her to take a seat. Spencer chose the chair beside hers.

"We have a… development."

"Concerning?"

"Drake Langston."

Blue outlined the situation with little embellishment. Ross listened in silence. A perfect poker face, she couldn't tell what he was thinking.

"I assume you're here representing Langston?"

"That's right," Spencer nodded.

"Hmm."

Ross rubbed a hand over his face. A knock on the door interrupted whatever he was about to say.

"Come in."

Vance Sutter stuck his head in the door.

"Well? I said come in. That means all the way."

"I'm sorry, Mr. Burton." Vance shot Blue a wary look. "I just heard about the meeting."

"Do you want to fill him in, or should I?" Ross didn't wait for Blue to answer. "Drake Langston is gay. He plans on telling the world this afternoon. An ex-lover. Blackmail. Not wanting to live under the burden. Blah, blah, blah. Does that about cover it?"

"Yes, sir."

Other than the multiple sarcastic blahs, Blue admired the way Ross boiled down the facts to a few succinct sentences.

"Well, we have to stop him," Vance erupted, wiping the sweat from his upper lip. Without a jacket, his fresh-that-morning shirt was already soaked under his arms. "Isn't there a morality clause in his contract?"

"One that covers drugs, woman-beating, and murder. Sexual orientation no longer applies."

"Why not?"

"Because this is the twenty-first century." Blue gripped the sides of her chair. Otherwise, she might give into the impulse and smack Vance's reddened face.

"Is there any chance of delaying Langston's coming out?" Unlike Vance, Ross was calm and pragmatic. "Until we can figure out the potential damage."

"Mr. Burton." At the moment, Blue was his employee, not his friend. She addressed him accordingly. "Drake *will* come out today."

"Talk him out of it," Vance yelled.

"I can't. Nor would I try. He didn't make this decision lightly. Blackmail is ugly. And, in case you've forgotten, illegal."

"True," Ross nodded sagely. "We can't risk sounding like we

condone such behavior."

"We can't risk sounding like we condone perversity. We cater to families, Mr. Burton. Do you think Mom and Dad will want to bring little Suzy and Bobby to watch a...?"

"A what?" Spencer asked, his eyes pinning Vance like a bug.

"I don't know the politically correct word," Vance waved his hand dismissively.

"Gay man. Homosexual. Take your pick."

Blue could see the desire in Spencer's eyes to knock Vance across the room. She'd had the same impulse more than once. But right now, the man and his prejudices didn't matter. Only one opinion counted.

"What do you say, Mr. Burton?"

Saved by the buzz. Ross looked more than a little relieved as he reached across his desk, hitting the intercom button. He knew damn well the delay was temporary. But any port in a storm.

"What!"

"I'm sorry to interrupt, Mr. Burton. Riley Preston is here to see you."

"Did we have an appointment?"

"No, sir. She—"

"Sorry to barge in, Ross." Riley burst through the door, Ross' assistant at her heels. "I thought you might like another owner's input."

"How did you hear?"

"A little bird." Riley smiled at Spencer when he gave her his chair. Crossing her long legs, her skirt showing just the right amount of skin for an early morning meeting, she set her lilac-colored Marc Jacobs handbag on the floor.

"Let me guess the *little bird's* name," Vance sneered.

"Blue called me for advice," Riley freely admitted. "The decision to crash your meeting was all my own."

"I appreciate the sentiment," Ross said, though his expression belied his words. "But this really doesn't concern you."

"I disagree. The Seattle sports community is a family. Didn't you say that in a speech just last week?"

"That sounds like me," Ross sighed.

Riley's eyes twinkled. "Face the facts, Ross. You can't prevent the inevitable. If you agree, a few of the Knights' players, current and ex, would like to attend Drake Langston's press conference."

"You're kidding." Blue couldn't keep her comment to herself. "Who?"

"Logan." Riley shrugged. "Sean and Gaige Benson are shooting a movie in Vancouver. But when I told them, they hopped on a private jet. They should land any minute."

Logan Price, Gaige Benson, and Riley's husband, Sean McBride. An impressive trifecta of Seattle sports royalty. Football Gods. For one of the few times in her life, Blue found herself speechless.

"I appreciate this, Riley." Apparently, Ross—with a big push from Riley Preston—had made up his mind. "I owe you."

"Any other time, I'd agree. But standing up for a man's right to love who he chooses, should have nothing to do with quid pro quo." Riley laid her hand on Blue's arm. "We're doing what's right. Which is sad. Because we shouldn't have to."

"Are you really going to let this happen?" Vance rounded on Ross, outraged beyond the point of self-preservation.

"Do you really have the balls to get in my face?" Ross rose, towering over his shorter, slighter employee.

"Mark my words. If you allow a little fag to dictate how you do things? The season? The team? Ashes."

"That's it."

Jumping to his feet, Spencer lunged at Vance. Showing amazing speed for a man his size, Ross put his considerable bulk between the two men.

"Tempting as the thought may be, I can't let my star player annihilate my ex-head of PR."

"Ex?" The zealot outrage seeped from Vance's body.

"You've made your position clear, Sutter. I have to assume working for a team with an openly gay player would be too much for you. Morally speaking."

"But—"

"Clear out your office."

As the reality of his situation sank in, green slowly replaced the red color suffusing Vance's face. He opened his mouth, but nothing came out.

"Now, Sutter."

When Vance was gone, Ross straightened his jacket, calmly walked around his desk, and dropped into his seat.

"That leaves the ball in your court. I hope you're ready for the shit storm to come."

"Me?" Blue's eyes widened.

"Vance is gone. Who else?"

"I assumed you would hire someone to take his place."

Ross shrugged. "Head of PR would always be your job to win or lose. I regret throwing you to the wolves so soon. But you brought me this situation, Ms. O'Hara. Handle it. Unless you don't think you're up to the task."

Blue's shoulders squared. Questioning her abilities was like waving a red flag in front of a bull. The gesture not only got her attention but made her determined to prove herself.

"I won't let you, or the team, down, Mr. Burton."

"I have no doubt," he said, reaching for his phone. "We have a lot to do before the press conference. You to coordinate the media and I," Ross let out a heavy sigh. "My board of directors will shit bricks. But, what the hell. We'll use them to build a barbecue in the bullpen. Give the relief pitchers something to do besides sitting on their thumbs."

"Thank you," Blue hugged Riley as soon as they were out of Ross' office. "Your arrival turned the tide."

"I don't know about that. You had plenty of backup without me."

"I'm very lucky to have so many good people in my life."

Blue took Spencer's hand. Her mind was already on what she had to do, who she had to call, and how she would get everything done in a few short hours. As a result, she missed the flare of pleased surprise in his eyes at her public gesture of affection.

But Riley noticed. She winked at Spencer. And he grinned back.

"You need to get going." Riley looked at her watch. "My troops are probably cleaning up as we speak. I need to text Sean to let him know the dress code. He'd kill me if I let Spencer show him up."

Spencer, his hand still in Blue's, walked her to her office.

"Do your magic," he told her. "Shoot me the details, and I'll make sure Drake and my gang are here on time."

Touching Spencer's face, Blue gave herself a moment before the crazy began.

"Your gang?"

"Nick and Travis."

Blue smiled. "Naturally."

"Before I came here, we had an emergency team meeting."

Spencer *had* been busy. "How did it go?"

"As you'd expect. Some of the guys jumped right on. Others were a bit more hesitant. A few...?" Spencer sighed.

"Vance isn't alone in his views."

"No. At least nobody vocalized their objections." Eyes narrowing, Spencer moved the edge of Blue's blouse to the side. His finger ran along the chain, coming to a stop at the cluster of sapphires. "You kept my gift."

"At least a dozen times I was so close to giving the necklace to one charity or another. Something always stopped me."

"Bluebell." Taking her hand, Spencer raised it to his lips. "Thank you for giving me a second chance."

"Thank you for asking."

If Spencer hadn't come back into her life, would Blue have spent the rest of her life subconsciously wondering what if? What if he hadn't broken up with her? What if they were still together? Would she have been happier with him? Or was she better off without?

Thankfully, she'd never have to find out.

"Do you want me to send in Peri?" Spencer asked, leaning close to brush a kiss across her cheek.

"Please."

Alone, Blue set aside her personal thoughts to concentrate on the job at hand.

"You updated the media file when? Last week?" Blue inquired the second Peri appeared.

"Pull up the list."

Blue gave Peri an abbreviated rundown. Without blinking, the woman got to work. Knowing the task was in capable hands, she finished the draft of Drake's statement that she'd started around five that morning.

Not bad. A few tweaks. A little polish. Attaching the final product to an email, she wrote:

Drake.

Read this carefully. I hope I've captured what you want to say, but DO NOT trust me with your words. Have your agent go over every letter with a fine-tooth comb. If there's anything you want to add or delete, let me know right away.

Remember. You have the power. Don't let anybody take even the slightest bit from you.

Crossing her fingers, Blue hit send.

"Which conference room do you want to use?"

Blue didn't ponder the question long. Only one choice made sense.

"First floor, east end."

Peri nodded her approval. "The biggest one available."

"One time only." Again, Blue crossed her fingers. "After today, Drake will deal with the press in smaller numbers. Hopefully, after a week or so, they'll be satisfied to let his skills on the baseball field do the talking for him."

BLUE PAUSED OUTSIDE the boardroom to catch her breath. T-minus twenty minutes and counting. The time had flown. Now, each second seemed to take an eternity.

Entering the room, Blue reminded herself not to let the fangirl in her spill over. Riley had introduced Sean, Logan, and Gaige when they first arrived. The fact that their wives were with them helped. The women humanized the men, bringing them off their pedestals—just a bit.

But at heart, Blue was a fan. She'd followed Gaige and Sean until they retired. She still watched every game Logan played. They were friendly. Approachable. And drop-dead gorgeous.

Blue wouldn't be human if she didn't get a bit of a thrill standing so close to her heroes.

"Everything is set," Blue said, automatically seeking out Drake. He looked a bit frazzled but strong. "How are you holding up?"

"Good. Really," he said when Blue raised a brow. "These last minutes seem like they're taking forever."

"I was thinking the same thing."

When Drake smiled, his dark hair slicked back, freshly shaven, he looked about sixteen years old. More than ever, Blue wished she could shield him from… everything.

Despite the baby-faced innocence he projected, Drake was a grown man. Strong and—Blue had to believe—capable of facing whatever came his way.

"Just a few more minutes," she assured him.

"May I see you outside?"

Blue started, unaware that Peri stood beside her.

"I'll be right back." Blue signaled for Spencer to follow her.

"Is there a problem?" she asked when the boardroom door shut behind them.

"Vance Sutter's assistant texted me. He's minutes away from sending out an email blast outing Drake."

Before Peri finished, Blue set off at a run. If the elevator hadn't arrived just as she did, she'd been prepared to lose her shoes and sprint up five flights of stairs.

"What the hell does he think he'll accomplish?" Spencer asked.

"He isn't thinking." Elevator or stairs, Blue figured she was faster without the heels. She slipped them off. "Vance is smart enough to understand that in the long run, his actions won't change anything. He's a gnat. But an annoying one. Drake deserves the right to deliver his message in his way. I'm not letting Vance take that from him."

Blue sprinted through the elevator doors. Spencer beat her by a few steps, leading the way into the office at the end of the hall. Head down, Vance typed furiously.

Grabbing the keyboard, Blue tossed it across the room. Vance surged to his feet, fist clenched.

"Goddamned bitch. Everything is your fault."

Vance swung wildly, not even close to hitting Blue. But Spencer wasn't taking any chance. His fist didn't miss.

"Nice shot," Gaige Benson said, strolling into the room. Cool, calm, and collected. The same way he played quarterback for almost twenty years. "We tossed a coin to see who would act as backup. I guess I wasn't needed."

"Too easy," Spencer said, standing over Vance's crumpled, unconscious body. "Do me a favor. Pick the asshole up so I can hit him again."

"Sorry," Gaige chuckled. "But if he makes another move, I won't stand in your way."

Blue looked at the clock.

"The press conference starts in five minutes."

"Your very efficient assistant has things under control," Gaige assured Blue. "Breathe. You've done everything you can. Above and beyond. The rest is out of your hands."

"I like things in my hands," Blue muttered.

"Here." Spencer handed Blue her shoes, happy to let her lean on him as she slid them on. "Listen to the old man."

"Hey," Gaige protested. "Forty-five is the new thirty."

Spencer chuckled, ignoring his friend.

"Ready?" Spencer held out his arm.

"Ready."

Flanked by Spencer on her left and Gaige on her right, Blue and the men took the elevator down to the first floor.

Please, Blue breathed deeply. In and out. *Let this work.* For herself. For the team. But mostly, for Drake Langston. He'd put his trust in her. She hoped she hadn't let him down.

CHAPTER EIGHTEEN

PEACE AND QUIET. After the whirlwind chaos of the past thirty hours, Blue would never take silence for granted again.

Wrapped in a blanket, and nothing else, Blue stared out the window at the sparkling waters of Lake Washington. The sun had just started to crest the top of Mt. Rainier. As views went, she couldn't think of a more spectacular venue to watch the day begin.

Why would Blue want to be anywhere but here? With Spencer sleeping safe and sound in the bed behind her.

Because having him so near was still a new feeling, Blue glanced over her shoulder—just to be sure. Yup. There he was. Spencer Kraig. Baseball player extraordinaire. Her friend. Her confidant. Her lover. Her hero.

And, quite possibly the best man she'd ever known.

The support Spencer showed Drake. The way he rallied the Cyclones to back their teammate. If she hadn't loved him before, his actions would've pushed her over the edge.

Blue could still see Spencer and the other men standing tall behind Drake during the press conference. Giving the young man their support for the whole world to see.

Drake handled himself admirably. Visibly nervous, he grew stronger with each passing minute. He stood taller. His voice firm. The barrage of flashing lights and overlapping questions threw him—briefly. But he rolled with the punches. Blue wanted to kiss him. Which she did as soon as they were away from prying eyes.

The stadium was packed with supportive fans. Whatever Drake had expected, he seemed stunned by the cheers that greeted him as he took the field. These were the Cyclone faithful. Ready to love their players no matter what.

On the road would be different. A story yet to be told.

Drake told Blue that he believed he made the right choice. That a weight had been lifted from his shoulders. He was ready to deal with the highs—and lows—of living life on his terms.

"What are you doing over here?" Spencer's arms closed around Blue, his lips nuzzling the side of her neck. "Instead of in bed with me?"

"Look." Blue nodded to where the sun was now in full view.

"Mm. Pretty. But not as pretty as you." Snaking his hand under the blanket, he cupped her breast.

Blue sighed. One magic touch. Turning, she enveloped Spencer under the cover, his hard, naked body better, warmer than the most expensive quilt.

"Somebody's up and ready for action."

"I need to make up for last night. All sleep and no action."

"You earned your rest," Blue assured Spencer, her lips tracing the tasty expanse of his chest. "You sat up all night with Drake. Met the press head on. And to top things off? Played a full nine-inning baseball game, followed by another round of interviews. I don't know how you managed to stay on your feet long enough for me to get you home."

"Sheer will. A hefty dose of determination. And a need to win. Which we did."

On the field and off. In a perfect, big-screen, Technicolor, Hollywood ending, Drake would've hit a home run to win the game. He and the Cyclones had to settle for him going two for four, a run scored, and a stellar defensive play.

Not exactly a fairy tale. But not bad. Not bad at all.

"Drake survived yesterday. The world didn't come to an end. The team didn't implode."

Blue stared into Spencer's eyes. In the morning light, the emerald green glistened bright and pure.

"Can you see October?"

Spencer shook his head. "I can see you. Right now? That's all that matters."

"I love you."

"Thank God." Spencer's kiss made Blue's head spin. "Because if you didn't, the next few moments would be a disaster."

"What—?"

Spencer dropped to one knee.

Blue's hand, the one that wasn't held in Spencer's covered her mouth. Eyes wide, she watched as he produced a ring with a simple platinum band and a square cut stone. Not a sapphire. Or an emerald.

"A diamond," Blue laughed.

Smiling, Spencer shrugged. "Seemed appropriate."

"I love you, Blue. Four years ago, I wasn't ready. But I am now. All in. With all my heart. Will you marry me?"

"I wasn't ready four years ago," Blue echoed Spencer's words with matched sincerity. "But I am now. All in. With all my heart. Yes, I'll marry you."

"Perfect fit," Spencer said, slipping the ring on her finger

Blue sank to her knees and into Spencer's waiting arms.

They'd taken a few detours. Hit more than a few bumps. And come out the other side. Together. Stronger than ever.

A perfect fit indeed.

EPILOGUE

LATE OCTOBER

In all of sports, nothing compared to game seven of the World Series.

Unless the scenario read as follows. Bottom of the ninth. The Cyclones behind by one. Runners on first and third. Spencer Kraig at the plate, the count three balls, and two strikes.

The game, the series—the entire season—was on the line. There was nobody the screaming fans or his nail-biting teammates would rather have up to bat. Yoda. The man with ice water in his veins. Mr. Clutch.

Locked into the moment, Spencer tuned out the screaming voices. He knew what was at stake. That elusive championship. A height few players ever achieved.

Signaling to the umpire for a timeout, Spencer stepped from the batter's box. He wasn't thinking home run. A single would tie the game. Drake was at first; with his speed, he'd likely score on a double.

Just a ball to the gap. That was all they needed.

As he adjusted his batting gloves, Spencer's gaze moved to the crowd on the third-base side. Three rows back. Blue. Wanting to experience every moment, she'd chosen to sit in the stands instead

263

of the owner's box.

Unlike the people around her, she wasn't jumping or yelling. She waited patiently. The look in her eyes telling him that she was there. Always, no matter what.

Just as Spencer was about to turn away, she shouted, her voice magically rising above all others. "What are you waiting for, Kraig? Win the damn game!"

Grinning, Spencer took his stance, raised his bat, and waited. He saw the ball leave the pitcher's hand as if in slow motion. The rotation was clear. The stitching a bright, glowing red. Slider. Middle of the plate. Maybe a little outside.

The hell with a double. That ball had home run written all over it.

Spencer swung for the fences. The crack of the bat told him he got all of it. The crowd rose to their feet. His teammates gathered on the top step of the dugout. As one, they watched as the ball soared.

Going. Going. Gone.

Throwing his arms in the air, Spencer didn't take the usual home run trot. He sprinted. Careful to touch each base. Rounding third, he found Blue. What a sight. She glowed. Screaming her lungs out, hugging strangers, blowing him kisses.

God. He loved that woman.

More than baseball. More than winning. More than anything.

Jumping on home plate, Spencer was swarmed by his teammates. They lifted him onto their shoulders, their jubilation something to behold.

Yes, Blue was the most important thing in his life. But at the moment, a world championship came pretty damn close.

Knowing his Blue, her love for him, and her love of the game, Spencer didn't doubt for a second that she'd understand.

COMING IN JUNE

FOR ANOTHER DAY

ONE STRIKE AWAY BOOK TWO

www.ingramcontent.com/pod-product-compliance
Lightning Source LLC
Chambersburg PA
CBHW071126170626
46809CB00002B/518